True-of-Voice

"That big one. Gray with white belly. Coming toward them. Think he is True-of-Voice," murmured Thistle-chaser.

Thakur studied the distant shape. It was definitely male, huge and heavy-shouldered, with a ruff. Deep gold eyes stared out of a wide gray face streaked with black.

"Why do you think he is True-of-Voice?"

"Song said he was. Before, when I heard it . . . Hard to explain, Thakur."

If the figure was not True-of-Voice, he was some sort of leader, for everyone drew aside and crouched out of his way. Was it because they feared him?

Thakur remembered the tyrant, Shongshar, who had forced Ratha out of the clan and then ruled it heartlessly. Ratha had had to kill him to free the Named and win back her leadership. Was this True-of-Voice another of the same breed?

FIREBIRD
WHERE FANTASY TAKES FLIGHT™

RATHA'S CHALLENGE

THE FOURTH BOOK OF THE NAMED

CLARE BELL

FIREBIRD

AN IMPRINT OF PENGUIN GROUP (USA) INC.

FIREBIRD

Published by the Penguin Group

Penguin Group (USA) Inc., 345 Hudson Street, New York, New York 10014, U.S.A.

Penguin Group (Canada), 90 Eglinton Avenue East, Suite 700,
Toronto, Ontario, Canada M4P 2Y3 (a division of Pearson Penguin Canada Inc.)

Penguin Books Ltd, 80 Strand, London WC2R 0RL, England

Penguin Ireland, 25 St Stephen's Green, Dublin 2, Ireland
(a division of Penguin Books Ltd)

Penguin Group (Australia), 250 Camberwell Road, Camberwell, Victoria 3124, Australia
(a division of Pearson Australia Group Pty Ltd)

Penguin Books India Pvt Ltd, 11 Community Centre,
Panchsheel Park, New Delhi - 110 017, India

Penguin Group (NZ), 67 Apollo Drive, Rosedale, North Shore 0745, Auckland, New Zealand
(a division of Pearson New Zealand Ltd.)

Penguin Books (South Africa) (Pty) Ltd, 24 Sturdee Avenue,
Rosebank, Johannesburg 2196, South Africa

Registered Offices: Penguin Books Ltd, 80 Strand, London, WC2R 0RL, England

First published in hardcover in the United States of America by Atheneum
(A Margaret K. McElderry Book), 1994
Published by Firebird, an imprint of Penguin Group (USA) Inc., 2007

1 3 5 7 9 10 8 6 4 2

LIBRARY OF CONGRESS CATALOGING-IN-PUBLICATION DATA

Bell, Clare.

Ratha's challenge : the fourth book of the Named / Clare Bell.

p. cm.

Summary: An encounter with a group of unusual cats helps bring Ratha, leader
of the prehistoric cat clan called the Named, and her estranged daughter,
Thistle, to a better understanding of each other.

ISBN 978-0-14-240915-2

[1. Cats—Fiction. 2. Mothers and daughters—Fiction. 3. Fantasy.] I. Title.
PZ7.B3889153Rasc 2007 [Fic]—dc22 2007015350

ISBN 978-0-14-240915-2

Printed in the United States of America

RATHA's
CHALLENGE

CHAPTER 1

STONES FLEW OVER Thakur's head and rattled against the bark of a tree behind him. The steep-sided gully in which he and his companions were trying to capture a shaggy young mammoth had become a trap for them instead of for the mammoth. Thakur crouched, flattening his fur and ears. The beast before him raised its trunk in a trumpeting blast.

Thakur drove his claws into the ground and bared his fangs in a feline hiss before he could stop himself. As herding teacher to his people, the Named, Thakur knew and taught the young ones all the skills that had been developed to manage dapplebacked horses and three-horn deer. He told his cub-students never to show fear to a herdbeast. Now he had broken his own rule, though this woolly tusker wasn't one of the clan's herdbeasts. Not yet.

The ground vibrated beneath Thakur's paws as the mammoth stamped its massive front feet and bellowed. The gully resounded with the brassy roar. His head ringing from the noise, Thakur glanced at his young fellow stalkers, Khushi and Bira.

Khushi, a herder, and Bira, a Firekeeper, had come

with him on this scouting expedition far from the clan's seacoast settlement. Khushi was a seasoned herder and not easily intimidated. This creature had him bristling all over. The usually calm Bira had a line of raised red-gold fur down her back.

This was their second attempt to catch a mammoth. And this one wasn't even fully grown—that was why they had chosen it.

Thakur and Khushi made another sharp rush at the beast, trying to back it into a narrow corner of the gully. Bira joined in. The quarry tossed its head, flailing its trunk and spearing the air with its tusks. Thakur's nose was filled with its heavy smell and the faint but sharp odor that told him that his two companions were fighting fear of their own. The beast's red-rimmed eyes glared from behind a thicket of orange hair. Its trunk swung down and coiled like a snake in the loose gravel. When the trunk whisked up again, another barrage of rocks hurtled at Bira.

She dodged, but several struck her ribs and back. Thakur heard her grunt in surprise and pain. Herdbeasts weren't supposed to throw rocks.

"You said this would be easier than herding three-horns!" Bira yowled at Khushi.

"I . . . thought . . . it would be since . . . these face-tail things . . . don't have horns!" Khushi puffed.

"They don't need them!"

Thakur glanced at Khushi. Every hair of the young herder's dun-colored fur was standing on end. Still, Khushi advanced on the quarry, trying to trap its gaze with his own. The stare-down worked on deer and dapplebacks, but this mountain of hide and flesh was having none of it.

With an enraged roar, the beast charged Khushi. Thakur and Bira both leaped at the same instant, snarling, to turn it back before it trampled him. They broke the face-tail's attack, but it would not be deprived of its quarry. Again the trunk swept down, but instead of gathering and flinging stones, it curled around Khushi's middle.

In an instant the squalling herder was lifted high over Thakur's head. Then he was shooting through the air. With a loud crash he landed in a thicket.

"Enough!" Thakur yowled to Bira, who was vainly trying to force the beast back to its corner with short rushes and feints. "Let the thing go!"

Bira dived to one side while Thakur galloped to the bush where Khushi had landed. He whirled, fearing for an instant that the beast would charge into the thicket and tear it apart trying to find Khushi. Even in his short experience with these animals, Thakur had found them to be very single-minded, especially when they wanted to trample an enemy.

With a ground-shaking trot, the orange-haired young mammoth headed for the thicket, then swerved aside. It lumbered away down the gully, ears flapping, short tail stuck stiffly upright.

Bira's ribs lifted in a sigh of combined exhaustion and relief. The red-gold fur on her back flattened, but worry remained in her green eyes. Thakur shared it. The face-tail had thrown Khushi hard.

"He's young and tough," Thakur said before Bira

could speak, but he could not keep anxiety out of his own voice as he pawed at the thicket, calling to Khushi.

At last he heard the herder's low moan. "Oooh, why did we try to catch that creature? I wish we had never seen it!"

Thakur's ears and whiskers lifted. Khushi couldn't be badly hurt if he chose to complain about the face-tail instead of about his own injuries.

Thakur and Bira turned to the task of extricating the herder. Only one of his feet was visible, hanging forlornly from a tangle of thorn scrub. Using claws and teeth, Thakur and Bira attacked the bush.

"Let me get Biaree," Bira offered as Thakur grimaced at the sharp twigs and thorns that lodged painfully between his teeth. He agreed. Bira ran off to fetch her treeling companion. Treelings were much better than the Named at untangling or clearing away things. Their clever fingers could do what paws and teeth could not.

Thakur thought longingly of his own treeling, Aree. His neck still felt bare without her small arms about it and her fingers twining in his fur. He'd left her behind in the clan's care, for she was bulging with babies. A mammoth-capturing expedition was no place for a pregnant treeling.

Soon Bira galloped back with her male treeling, Biaree, perched on the nape of her neck. The treeling's slender ringed tail stuck up, and a pointed light-brown muzzle with a black mask showed between Bira's ears. A few purrs of encouragement and a nudge from Bira's nose soon had the treeling pulling apart branches and breaking off dead twigs. With his aid, they cleared a way in to Khushi and gently pulled him out.

Khushi was more shaken than hurt. While Bira and Biaree groomed thorns and twigs from the young herder's hide and tail, Thakur used his paws and his sensitive nose to check Khushi for injuries.

"Why did I ever tell the clan leader about these animals that wear their tails on their faces?" Khushi asked him plaintively. "And why did I ever think we could add them to our herds?"

"I think we will be able to, when we find ways to manage them," Thakur answered.

"If we ever do." Khushi groaned.

Thakur didn't contradict him. Despite his words, he wasn't sure that these beasts the Named called face-tails would work out as herd animals. There was certainly a lot of meat on one, but Khushi's unexpected trip through the air had shown that there were certain hazards involved in taming them.

"Well," said Bira, "if they aren't suitable, it won't be the first time we've chosen the wrong kind of animal. Thistle's seamares didn't work out either."

As he watched Bira and Biaree finish grooming Khushi, Thakur licked his own dark-copper fur and thought of their previous attempt to bring a new kind of animal into the herd. Last season's drought and its effects on the three-horn deer and dapplebacked horses had made Ratha, the clan leader, start the search. If the clan herds had animals that could survive under different kinds of conditions, the Named would have a more stable supply of meat.

Ratha's idea was a good one, but putting it into practice was difficult. It had also yielded one very unexpected result. While scouting the seacoast for possible herdbeasts, Thakur had found a crippled young female of his own kind. She turned out to be Thistle-chaser, Ratha's lost daughter.

Thakur had also found the seamares, chunky water creatures with horselike heads and webbed feet—and tusks that they used to dig up and tear apart heavy-shelled clams on the shore. Thistle had formed a strange but real friendship with them. When the clan tried to capture and keep seamares, she angrily interfered. Then she turned her wrath against her mother.

Thakur still remembered finding the two on the wave-washed rocks, both bleeding from their fight and nearly dead from exposure. Since then Ratha and her daughter had become partially reconciled, but Thistle had not accepted Ratha's offer to join the clan. She remained apart, living among the seamares.

With a twitch of his whiskers, Thakur turned his attention back to Khushi, who had recovered enough to shake the last leaves and twigs out of his coat.

"Maybe you should have used a lighted torch," he heard Khushi say to Bira. "I haven't seen a beast yet who didn't fear the Red Tongue."

Except us and our treelings, Thakur thought. And I have seen that we do fear it, although in a different way than the herdbeasts.

"Thakur doesn't like using the Red Tongue to frighten herdbeasts," Bira said, looking to him. "I agree. It's cruel and often useless. Once a herdbeast is maddened by fear, you can't do anything except kill it. That is a waste."

"And imagine what would have happened if that face-tail had grabbed the torch and flung it," Thakur said, entering the conversation. "If it hadn't hit one of us, it would have spread the Red Tongue all over the grass."

"That wretched beast deserved to get burned up," Khushi growled.

"Yes, and we'd have burned up with it," Bira reproved. "You know how fast the Red Tongue can run."

Khushi admitted that they were right, but he wouldn't have minded if Bira had singed the obnoxious mammoth in a tender spot.

"I need to see that the embers in the fire-den haven't gone out," Bira announced, lifting her plumed tail. "Are we going back to the knoll? Good, I'll meet you there."

As she loped off down the gully, Thakur climbed up the side, followed by Khushi. He found the hill that they had used as a vantage point to locate the face-tails. It had a single oak that gave shade from the sun. The prevailing breeze carried their own scent away from the face-tail herd.

It brought him the odors of many other kinds of animals. Among these were feline scents that might belong to the Un-Named outsiders who outwardly resembled his own people but had only the minds and ways of beasts. Everything was so overlaid with the pungent smell of mammoth that Thakur could not be sure. He was not going to worry. The Red Tongue that Bira carried would protect him and his party.

He sat down in the litter of last season's leaves and acorns, letting his gaze travel over the rolling plain below. It was still filled with the face-tailed beasts, some wallowing in a marshy sink between two hills, some drifting back and forth in a large group as they tore up grass with their trunks and stuffed it into their mouths.

The young ones showed up as blotches of orange against the more somber black and brown wool of their elders.

One of those orange splotches was probably the animal that had just escaped them. Despite their bulk the face-tails could move fast. Thakur eyed the beasts, trying to pick one that was young enough to be vulnerable and old enough not to need the protection of its mother. It wasn't easy. Yesterday he had chosen a young calf and ended up fleeing from the enraged mother. Today's quarry had proved to be old enough to defend itself.

His ears pricked forward as a line of smaller shapes emerged from a copse of trees near the wallow. They were not face-tails, nor any other kind of herdbeast. Beside him he felt Khushi stiffen as the wind brought a stronger version of a familiar scent to their noses.

"Un-Named ones, Thakur!" Khushi hissed.

The herding teacher hesitated in his reply. Yes, the forms were the cat shapes that resembled those of his own kind, but never had he seen the Un-Named do what these newcomers were doing.

The line broke up as its members dispersed and melted into the high grass about the wallow. Thakur narrowed his eyes. At one end of the marshy area stood a face-tail whose patchy orange-and-black coat showed that it was older than the one the Named had tried to capture.

"They are hunting it," Bira said. She had arrived so quietly that Thakur had hardly noticed.

Yes, they were. He caught a glimpse of a circle of hidden stalkers creeping toward the face-tail. There were more hunters than he had first thought, and they seemed to move with a deadly purpose. Unconsciously he eased himself down, peering through the high grass. Bira and Khushi followed his example.

The face-tail, unconcerned, was sloshing in the wallow, squirting water over itself with its trunk. The circle of hunters paused, as if making the final decision to attack. The scent wafting to Thakur's nose carried more than a sense of hunger or the usual blind ferocity of the Un-Named. He sensed a certain unified purpose in their behavior that surprised him.

If these ones are truly Un-Named, they are different than any I know, he thought.

He did not see which individual triggered the attack. At one instant they were all crouched together in the grass; the next they were swarming onto the startled face-tail. Muddy water turned pink as the attackers clawed their way up the beast's flanks and laid open its flesh with deep slashes.

The rest of the face-tails, alarmed, lumbered away with raised trunks, abandoning the victim.

The struggle did not last long. Despite the face-tail's trumpeting and plunging, it soon toppled under the savagery of the assault. For a while it flailed in the shallow water as the hunters gathered atop it and began to feed. Then it grew still.

Beside him, Thakur felt Bira shivering. "I have never seen Un-Named ones like these before," she hissed. "And I don't like them!"

Khushi was struck silent. "They made it look . . . easy!" he blurted at last.

"Sh. We don't want to attract their attention," Thakur cautioned.

Bira began to creep slowly backward, deeper into the shade cast by the oak. Khushi followed. Thakur, torn between curiosity and fear, was the last to come away.

"Let's go," said Bira as Biaree huddled nervously on her shoulders.

Thakur agreed, but would only let his companions retreat as far as the small fire-den Bira had dug to store the coals of the Red Tongue.

He was thinking hard. The speed and efficiency of the unknown hunters told him that they were not a ragtag group of Un-Named ones such as those that had raided the clan's herds in previous seasons. Even the organized attacks that had nearly decimated the Named had not been as complex or as smoothly carried out as this hunt. His sense of danger told him to leave these hunters far behind, but there was another sense that told him to stay.

Who were they? Where had they come from? How had they learned to hunt such formidable prey as the face-tails? The questions whirled through Thakur's mind.

"You saw the hunt," he argued, when his two companions protested against the idea of remaining. "Something like that takes more than strength and fierceness. They were working together."

Bira gave him a questioning look. "The Un-Named *can* work together. They did when they attacked us several seasons ago."

"Yes, but those attacks were not as well planned as the hunt we just saw. I was in those fights. I remember." Thakur turned to Khushi. "This kill looked easy because everything was arranged in advance. Each hunter knew

exactly what she or he was supposed to do and did it."
He continued, growing more excited. "Don't you see?
Not only must they be able to think and speak, they
must be able to make detailed plans and describe them
to each other. They must be like us!"

The other two stared at him, their jaws hanging open.
As long as the Named had existed, they had thought
their clan was the only one of its kind and that they alone
had the gifts of awareness, forethought, and speech. A
few individuals with such gifts existed among the Un-
Named, but they had come from fringe matings with
the clan.

Perhaps the Named were not unique after all.

Thakur and his two companions returned to the scene
of the kill, hid, and watched patiently. The face-tail
hunters were joined by others: elders, half-grown cubs,
and nursing or pregnant females. The group all gorged
themselves until late in the day. They then scattered to
chew on bones they had taken from the carcass, or to
lie in the sun.

Now was the best time to approach, Thakur decided.
The Un-Named would be sated and sleepy. Carefully
he and the others crept to a small stand of brush that
was closer to the hunters and safely downwind.

"Are you sure this is a good idea, herding teacher?"
Bira asked when he told her what he planned and asked
her to stay behind with a small flame of the Red Tongue
and pine branches to light for torches.

"They won't attack. They've eaten too much. And if
they chase us, they can't run far with heavy stomachs."

Bira was still doubtful. She also questioned Thakur's

conviction that he would be able to talk to the face-tail hunters. "We did not hear them speak to each other," she argued quietly. "And they did not seem to be following a leader's directions. That tells me that they are not like us. Perhaps we should wait and keep watching from a distance."

Thakur answered that those objections had occurred to him, but that this chance was one worth taking. The hunters would only be sated and lazy for a short time. Afterward it would be too dangerous to approach.

Khushi, listening to them both, offered to go by himself. Thakur's skills were too valuable to risk losing, he said. Who else would instruct the clan's young if the herding teacher were killed?

"You and all the other herders I have trained," Thakur answered. "Together you have enough knowledge. What you do not have is my experience in dealing with strangers outside the clan. I don't plan to let myself be killed. You and I look enough like the hunters to fool them, at least from a distance."

"What about our smell?"

"Rolling in face-tail dung should disguise it; the stuff is strong enough."

Khushi only made a grimace.

Thakur gazed out over the open plain where the hunters sprawled in scattered groups. "Bira, watch us and keep a torch ready. I hope we will not need it. . . ."

"But if you do, the Red Tongue will be there," Bira said fiercely, taking up her post.

With Khushi pacing beside him, Thakur left the sheltering brush and walked out onto the open plain. The sun sat low behind him and the sky was starting to pale into the colors of dusk. After rolling thoroughly in a fresh pile of face-tail manure, he and Khushi took a wandering course toward the hunters. Sometimes the two lay down or even flopped over on their backs for a little while, imitating the bloated lassitude of the others.

The smell of the carcass was rich in Thakur's nose. Next to him, Khushi swallowed, and the aroma of hunger tinged his smell. Thakur could not blame the young herder. His own mouth was watering. They had eaten yesterday, a few ground-birds caught by Bira, but it was not enough to fill their bellies.

"Don't think about eating," he said when he saw the thought in Khushi's eyes. "We won't get close to the kill. The chances are that they will smell something strange about us, despite the dung, and chase us away."

To Thakur's astonishment, his deception worked. In the fading light the two managed to pass the outer fringes of the large group without being challenged. To one side, Thakur saw spotted cubs gamboling around their parents. He and Khushi skirted a group of half-grown males all snoring together in a pile.

"They don't even post sentries?" Khushi whispered to Thakur.

"Why should they? Who is going to attack them? As for the kill, it is too heavy to be stolen, and they have eaten all they want."

Thakur looked about for someone who might respond to their approach. He chose a group of three who were resting but not asleep. One was toying with a broken piece of rib bone, but none were still eating. As one lifted a muzzle against the sky, Thakur could see that the fangs were long enough to show outside the mouth.

The sight of those teeth reminded him of Shongshar, the orange-eyed stranger that Ratha had once taken into the clan. Could these hunters be his people? Feeling a chill, Thakur hoped not. Shongshar had turned into a tyrant, overthrowing Ratha and ruling the clan with his savage ways and long saber-teeth. One of his kind was enough.

But the fangs of these hunters were not as long as Shongshar's, although their teeth were longer than Thakur's own. The length seemed to vary in different individuals. It also did among the Named, although not to such extremes.

He realized that he was delaying, fearful of making the first try at speaking to these people. Was he more afraid of provoking an attack or of losing his hope that this group might be a clan like the Named? He did not know.

"Khushi, stay close behind me and don't say anything," he warned. His mouth, wetted by appetite, went dry with apprehension. His usually eloquent tail felt stiff and clumsy. Swallowing to moisten his tongue, he deliberately approached the other group. Eyes—green, gold, and amber—shone in the fading dusk.

He feared that his heart was booming loud enough for everyone to hear. His pelt felt as though it would jump right off his body—every hair was standing so much on end. Would the face-tail hunters know him for a stranger and attack, or would they welcome him as a brother?

Not trusting the manure scent to conceal his smell

entirely, he and Khushi positioned themselves down-wind of the three they were approaching. He lifted his tail in a friendly arch.

One, a tawny female with heavy shoulders, got up. He was afraid she would snarl, but instead she extended her muzzle for a nose-touch. His hopes leaped up. This was the same greeting the Named knew and used. Eagerly he answered in kind, breathing in her scent. It was much like that of his own people, though overlaid with the powerful aroma of face-tail.

The two others in the group roused themselves and also greeted him with the nose-touch. One even rubbed a welcoming chin on Thakur's shoulder and flopped a tail across his back. Khushi was also accepted.

Yet as soon as the nose-touching and rubbing were finished, the three turned back to lazing or grooming or playing, without a word to the newcomers. Thakur found this disconcerting. They must have recognized that he was a stranger. Why, then, hadn't they attacked him or chased him away?

Or, if for some reason they had chosen to accept him anyway, why wouldn't they say something to him?

He rolled over on his side, nudging Khushi to follow suit. He would have to speak first. A dismaying thought seized him. He had not heard any of these hunters talk. Suppose Bira was right and they couldn't.

No, that can't be true, he argued to himself. They could not have organized that hunt if they couldn't tell each other what to do.

Perhaps their language was all gesture and scent. As Thakur considered that possibility, he heard a voice that was not Khushi's.

"Give the bone," it said. The heavy-shouldered female was trying to paw the rib fragment from the male
who was playing with it.

"No. Go get another. There are plenty left in the
carcass," came the irritable reply.

Thakur's heart leaped in excitement. Not only did
these ones speak, but they used a language so close to
that of the Named that he could understand what they
said. He waited tensely, hoping someone would speak
to him.

The female yawned. "The meat was tender."

"Salty," said the other.

"Go drink," the male advised. "There are places at
the water hole."

Thakur's ears, which had been sharply pricked,
started to sag. Surely they had more interesting things
to say than this. He made himself stay quiet and listen,
but he heard only more of the same.

Khushi, bored, yawned widely, showing all his teeth.
He snapped his mouth shut self-consciously.

"Open it again," said the male who was playing with
the bone. Thakur blinked when he realized the command had been given to Khushi. Khushi was startled,
too. Thakur had to nuzzle him before he responded.

The male peered into Khushi's mouth. "Those fangs
are too short. Stop eating bones. They wear teeth down.
The song says good teeth are needed for the hunt. Listen
to the song."

"The . . . song?" asked Khushi, but he spoke so softly
that the male didn't hear him. Thakur listened, but he
could hear nothing like the courting yowls the Named
called songs.

Puzzled, he asked the hunter, "What are you listening to?"

He thought he spoke clearly, but the male only gave him a baffled look. "Those words are confusing," the other said. "Speak again."

Thakur had no idea why his question was not clear. "The song," he faltered.

"The song is always being sung," the other stated.

"Why can't I—"

"Stop speaking!" the male ordered sharply. "Those words make no sense."

Puzzled and slightly irritated, Thakur closed his mouth. He noticed that the others in the group were eyeing him as if he were something noxious that had walked into their midst. What had he said? He wondered if it had been wise for him to confess he could not hear this "song" or whatever it was that they were making such a fuss about.

Perhaps if he stayed away from that, he might make some headway. With a sinking heart he realized that it was already too late. His easy acceptance and anonymity in the group were gone. Now he was the subject of attention and discussion.

"The ears don't work," said the female, looking at him with a grimace and turning to the male.

"The ears do work. The words are heard."

"The song is not heard." The female stared at Thakur with molten-gold eyes.

Without answering her stare directly, Thakur tried to get a good look into her eyes. He expected to meet a gaze that was much like his own. He felt the fur prickle up and down his tail when he could not find what he sought. The look in her eyes was neither the blank, unknowing stare of the animal-like Un-Named, nor the sharp, aware gaze of his own people. It was aware, yes, but the awareness was somehow . . . different.

"The song is heard," Thakur put in quickly, imitating the odd style of speech.

He hoped his answer would mollify the hunters, but the suspicion in the female's face grew deeper as she stared at him. "The form is not known to True-of-voice. The eyes are not known; the voice is not known."

What did she mean? Thakur could make no sense out of what she was saying. Perhaps True-of-voice was her name.

"True-of-voice," he repeated. "Is that you? Is True-of-voice your name?"

He did not know if she understood him or not, but he saw he had made a major blunder. She flattened her ears and spat.

The other hunters traded looks, bristled, and growled. Thakur noticed that the misunderstanding was starting to draw attention from groups outside their own.

He decided that the time had come to withdraw and think things out before he got himself and Khushi into more trouble. With a poke he got the young herder on his feet. They both backed away from the now-hostile hunters, turned, and jogged in the direction they had come.

Though no one had noticed their initial approach, heads now lifted and eyes followed as they passed. It was as if word of the intruders had somehow spread instantly throughout the group, even though Thakur had heard no cries of alarm.

"Don't run," he warned Khushi, even though the muscles in his own hindquarters were twitching with the impulse to turn tail and flee.

Only when he had put the group at a distance did he and Khushi break into a bounding run. It carried them to the bushes, where Bira met them.

"What happened?" she asked.

Thakur sighed. "I said something wrong. I don't know what."

"So they do speak like us?"

"They use words, but not the way we do. Bira, we had better not stay here. We're too close, and they're angry."

Quickly the Firekeeper packed up the coals in an old bird's nest filled with sand. Khushi helped, taking the resinous pine branches that served as firebrands.

Once Thakur decided they were a safe distance from the hunters, the Named made camp. Bira lit a fire from the embers she carried, and everyone drew close around it.

"I think we should give up on that bunch," said Khushi, disgusted. "They may speak, but they are as stupid as the Un-Named. And crazy too. They kept mewling about some song. I couldn't hear anyone singing. Could you, Thakur?"

"No," the herding teacher confessed. He was disappointed at his failure. Khushi's dismissal of the hunters as witless and crazy provided an easy escape from his own responsibility. For an instant he was tempted to take it. Perhaps no one could talk to these people. If so, he could not fault himself for failing.

Yet he knew the answer was not so simple. He had

been close enough to look into their eyes. He had seen an alertness there, not the blank unawareness of the Un-Named. But it was directed strangely inward in a way he did not understand.

And it echoed something that he had seen and knew well, though at first he could not think what it was. Then he remembered another pair of eyes, sea-green and once shrouded by pain. Those were Thistle's eyes when he had first found her.

He remembered how he had coaxed Thistle back outside herself, had given her not only words to speak with, but hope. How those eyes had begun to brighten and clear, showing that she was truly of the Named. Yet even now, her gaze would sometimes become opaque and she would retreat where none of the Named could follow. To Thakur it seemed as though Ratha's daughter walked two paths, one with the Named and another in a cave world of mist and entrancement, where strange voices echoed.

Voices. The hunters had spoken, in their puzzling way, of a voice, a song that Thakur could not hear. Perhaps only they could hear it. The one name they had said was True-of-voice. In some way speech was vital to them, yet why did their grasp of it seem so limited and stilted?

It was clear that they did not walk the same path as the Named. But there was one among the Named who might be able to follow them. Thakur sensed that he would never be able to speak to these hunters by himself. He needed Thistle.

But she was not a clan member and did not have to

obey Ratha or anyone else. If he sent for Thistle, the decision to come or not would be hers alone.

Was this the right thing to do? Thakur wondered. Would such a contact with the group of strange cats bring joy or disaster? The hunters could be a formidable enemy, but what if they were an allied clan who could help the Named survive?

He would send for Ratha as well as Thistle, he decided. Experienced as he was, he could not be alone in decisions that involved the future of the Named. Ratha must see these hunters for herself.

When the herding teacher came out of his reverie, he was slightly chagrined to find that Bira had banked the fire and that both she and Khushi had gone to sleep. Try as he would, Thakur could not close his eyes. He remained awake long into the night, thinking.

CHAPTER 2

DAYS LATER, WIND was kicking up sand on a coastal beach, stinging Thistle's eyes and nose. She felt lonely and cross, for her friend Thakur had been gone too long. The haze that had once clouded her mind came less often now, but today it was here, making her feel remote and withdrawn.

Keeping her claws fixed in the driftwood log, she pulled at her injured foreleg to make the muscles stretch, as Thakur had taught her. From a short distance away came a splintering sound. Ratha was using the same log to sharpen her claws.

Thistle could not help a glance sideways at her mother. Ratha was on top of the log, raking backward with the powerful muscles in her shoulders. Half fascinated, half resentful, Thistle watched. Ratha looked so beautiful and strong. She was all one tawny color that flowed over her head, down the bowed arch of her back, over her hindquarters, and out the long sweep of her tail.

Thistle wondered if anyone would ever watch *her* sharpening her claws and think that she was strong and beautiful. No. Even if her limp went away, she would still be small and awkward. And ugly, for her pelt was rusty black, mottled with orange.

She looked quickly away before Ratha could notice her gaze. The hard green light in her mother's eyes burned too brightly today. Only when those eyes were half-closed or dulled by suffering or illness did Thistle dare approach and touch or lick her mother. When Ratha was strong and well, Thistle kept her inside thoughts well hidden.

Thistle gazed down at her outstretched leg. It was much stronger now. She could almost walk without a limp along short paths. Soon she hoped she would be able to walk for short distances without a limp. The leg no longer hurt either. At least most of the time. Only when . . .

No. Thistle flattened her ears. She wasn't going to think about the Dreambiter that appeared to her in nightmares. Thinking about it could too easily bring it, as if thoughts were meat laid on a trail that it prowled. But not thinking sometimes brought it, too.

Today, for some reason, it was hard to think and hard not to think. The wind and blowing sand seemed to catch everything in her mind and whirl it away. She sank her claws deeper into the gray driftwood and stretched her leg muscles until she felt the good healing hurt that promised to make that leg, once shrunken and crippled, as sound as her other limbs.

She heard a yawning sound as Ratha opened her jaws and curled her tongue upward in pleasure. Thistle saw the white sharpness of her teeth. She remembered, before she could catch herself, that the nightmare also had such sharp teeth.

And the nightmare, thus summoned, came.

The Dreambiter's soft tread quickened, echoing along the caverns within Thistle's mind. Thistle's eyes and ears filled with blackness, and she felt herself being pulled deep into those caves. However she might struggle and scream and cry out, she could not break free. The sound of the Dreambiter's feet became louder and faster.

Dimly, a voice cried out from beyond the cave, but she couldn't understand it, for words had been lost to the rising howl of the Dreambiter. The blackness that was deeper and harder than anything outside pounced on her, green eyes flaming, mouth open, teeth bared. The upper fangs sank into her shoulder, the lower fangs into her chest, for she was suddenly small enough in the nightmare for her forequarters to fit within the Dreambiter's mouth.

With the shock came the flooding pain that raged from her shoulder and chest to her foreleg, drawing the leg up in a cramped knot. Writhing, screaming, she clawed at the Dreambiter with her good forepaw, but her foe was made of nothingness, and her claws found no hold. Then the jaws released her, but the release was almost worse than the bite, for when the teeth pulled out, it hurt more than ever, and the hurt flamed and seared until the pain burned away everything—herself, the caves, the Dreambiter—until all were ashes.

And the ashes were picked up by the wind and swirled high into the sky. They slowly drifted down.

Ratha yanked her claws from the driftwood as soon as she saw Thistle stiffen. She was beside her daughter in an instant, seeing the milky sea-green color of her eyes swirl, closing the pupils to points. With a jerk that freed her claws from the log, Thistle staggered backward on her hind legs, overbalanced, and fell on her back.

"Fessran!" Ratha yowled her friend's name, thanking the impulse that had drawn the Firekeeper leader to come with her on this visit to Thistle's beach. Fessran was a short distance down the beach, looking after Mishanti, the young cub Thistle had adopted. Ratha wished Thakur were there, but he was gone on the search for the face-tailed beasts.

Thistle's tail lashed the sand; her claws raked it. She writhed, hissed, and spat, striking with bared claws at an enemy only she could see. Then she screamed aloud with pain, and the foreleg she had been stretching pulled up against her chest and locked there, as if once again crippled and shrunken.

Ratha found her voice joining Thistle's wordless cries, as if she could drive the nightmare from her daughter by sheer force of rage. She caught Thistle by the scruff, trying to hold her gently and tenderly as if she were a small cub. When she and her brothers were small, Ratha had carried them that way. She remembered how the wiggling bodies relaxed in her jaws, for the cubs sensed that they were safe.

Thistle only struggled harder, wrenching Ratha's head back and forth. Ratha tried to soothe and calm her daughter with words, but her mouth was full of Thistle's fur.

Fessran galloped up, her sandy-colored coat blackened with streaks of soot from the fires she tended. Raising her voice above Thistle's squalling, Fessran yowled,

"Quit the mother stuff, Ratha. It doesn't work. The only thing to do is get her to the lagoon." With her jaws she seized Thistle at the root of the tail and began hauling her toward a briny pool that lay behind the upper beach. Ratha, her mouth full of fur and her head swimming from being jerked back and forth, followed Fessran's tugging.

Together they got Thistle over the sand and into the pool. Fearing that her daughter would drown while in the fit, Ratha held Thistle's head up, but Fessran told her to let go.

"She'll lift her nose to breathe. Just leave her alone. The water calms her. I don't know why, but it works."

Ratha knew that Fessran was right. As soon as the pool had wetted Thistle's flank, she relaxed and stopped fighting. Now she drifted, looking like an orange-splotched brown sea otter. Ratha waited to see that she did lift her nose to take breaths and only then did she leave her daughter and wade to shore with Fessran.

She permitted herself one angry swipe at the ripples crossing the lagoon, jealous that its waters could soothe Thistle when she could not. Then she shook herself hard, sending spray flying in all directions.

"Come on," said Fessran.

Ratha stayed silent, looking at Thistle.

Fessran nudged her. "I know you are angry. Be angry somewhere else."

Fessran's suggestion wasn't the most helpful, but Ratha couldn't think of an alternative. When they had gone a short distance from the pool, Ratha flopped down on her side. Wanting comfort, she wished she had her treeling, but she had left Ratharee safely hidden, just in case something like this should happen. Fessran sat down, curling her tail about her feet.

"She will be all right?" Ratha asked.

"Every time she gets one of those fits, Thakur drags her over and throws her in. Sometimes Thistle gets herself in when she feels it coming on. This one must have been too sudden."

Ratha lay, trying not to resent the fact that Fessran and Thakur knew more about Thistle than she did. Her tail flipped irritably.

"Are you angry at me?" Fessran asked.

"No."

"At her?"

"Yes and no. It isn't her fault that she has fits. Thakur says that now they don't come as often, but I hate seeing her in them. And when I come to visit, she seems uneasy."

"Well," said Fessran slowly, "it is still hard for her to be near you."

"If I were her I wouldn't want to be anywhere near me," Ratha said bitterly. "I wouldn't want to be near a mother who had attacked and bitten me for something I could not help. If I hadn't been so reckless and cruel . . ."

"Before you pull out more of your own fur," Fessran said, "let me tell you one thing."

"What?"

"Young ones can be stupid."

"That doesn't justify what I did. She might have been slow-witted, but—"

Fessran interrupted. "I'm not talking about Thistle. I'm talking about you. You had those cubs when you were scarcely more than a cub yourself." She paused. "You were young. Young ones can be stupid. They haven't had time to learn or they are too impatient. You bit Thistle because you were young. You are older now. You wouldn't do it again."

Ratha opened her mouth to make a retort, then closed it again. Fessran gave her a quizzical look and said, a bit smugly, "These things are all simple when you turn them around the right way. It's like learning to open a herdbeast carcass. You have to start at the right place."

"Only you would say it that way," Ratha grumbled, laying her nose on the sand.

"Only you would need to hear it that way, clan leader," Fessran answered lightly, nibbling crusted sand from one paw. "Do you feel better?"

"I should say I feel worse, just to spite you." Ratha eyed her friend. "But I do feel better."

Fessran stood up and shook herself off again, peering down the beach. Ratha remembered that she had been watching Mishanti while Thistle did her leg stretching.

"I made him sit down and told him to stay there," Fessran said. "I have no doubt that he is now tearing all over the beach. I am beginning to think that his ears have no connection to the inside of his head." With a sigh, she added, "I had better go and look for him."

"Wait," Ratha said as she saw a puff of dust rise from the cliff where the path ran down to the beach. "He might be up there." She stared harder. "No. That's someone else."

Fessran joined her in squinting at the path. "They're certainly in a hurry, judging by all the dust being kicked up. Or clumsy. No, both—that's my son Khushi up on the trail."

Khushi! Ratha had sent him off many days ago with Bira and Thakur to find the face-tailed beasts. What had happened to bring him back so soon? Her ears swiveled forward as she watched Khushi skitter around one bend after another on the switchbacks of the trail. Soon he was down on the beach, bounding over the dunes.

"Clan leader!" he cried as he slid to a stop. "Thakur sent me with a message."

"Is he well? Is Bira well?"

"Yes, they are both fine. We found the face-tailed beasts you sent us after. But we also found another tribe of clan-cats. That is why Thakur sent me back."

"Another clan like us?" Ratha stared at him.

Khushi's words spilled out in a breathless rush. "Well, Thakur thinks they may turn out to be like us, although they are hunters and not herders. He has been having trouble trying to talk to them, and that is why he wants you to come. He wants Thistle-chaser as well."

Ratha had him repeat the last part, not sure that she had heard him correctly. Thistle? Was Khushi sure that was who Thakur wanted?

"Yes. He made it very clear and he was very insistent. I don't know why he wants her, but he does."

Baffled, she asked Khushi other questions, all the while trying to figure out why Thakur wanted Thistle.

Unless he wants her there just because he is fond of her, Ratha thought. No. Thakur doesn't do things for those sorts of reasons.

Fessran spotted Mishanti far down the beach and took off after him, leaving Ratha standing beside Khushi.

"My mother," the young scout said with a grin. "She always complains about how much work it is to raise cubs, but she can't seem to live without at least one."

"One Mishanti is all anyone can manage." Ratha watched Fessran's efforts to corral the youngster. She began pacing down the beach, Khushi beside her. "How did Thakur find this other clan?"

"They were also hunting the face-tailed beasts."

"Are these strangers like us?"

"I don't think so, but they resemble us enough that Thakur and I were able to go in among them. They even have a language like ours. Thakur said he could understand their words."

"Then why couldn't he speak to them?" Ratha asked, puzzled.

"I don't know. They said things that made no sense. His replies only confused them and made them angry."

This surprised Ratha. Of all the Named, Thakur was the most sensitive and the least likely to commit a blunder that might offend a stranger.

They trotted up to Fessran, who was sitting on a squirming Mishanti. Khushi touched noses with his mother, but seeing that she was preoccupied, kept his greeting short.

Ratha told him to go back up to the cliff dens and get something to eat, for he looked hungry. At her words Khushi brightened and scampered back up the path. He was a good scout, Ratha thought. Even though he must have traveled a long way, he hadn't eaten before he came down to the beach to find her.

Fessran freed a rather flattened and rumpled Mishanti.

"You keep blaming yourself for Thistle's fits," she said to Ratha when Khushi was gone, "but I think this little scamp here is another cause. He must drive Thistle a bit wild. I can handle him, but I've had much more experience raising litters than Thistle."

"She *wanted* to adopt him," Ratha said.

"I know, and she is keeping to the agreement we made, but I know that she has been tempted to do more than sit on him. One thing she definitely has from you is your temper."

Ratha grimaced at her friend's bluntness. "She hasn't bitten him yet."

"No. She's the one who gets bitten. By that nightmare of hers." Fessran put a paw on the cub, who had started to creep away, tempted by some gulls nearby. "I told her that if she felt she was going to lose her temper with him, she should come to me. And she has. Several times. But I can't come to the beach as often, especially now in the rainy season. The Firekeepers need my help to keep the fires lit."

"She's not a clan member, Fessran," Ratha said in a low voice. "I can't order her to do anything, even if I feel it is for her own good."

"Well, she should get away from this little mischief maker, at least for a while. Tell her that I'll get someone to look after him so that you can take her to Thakur."

The tip of Ratha's tail twitched in annoyance. "I can't take her anywhere unless she chooses to go. I doubt if she will. She hates to leave the beach."

"Well, Thakur gave you quite a task, then, didn't he," said Fessran.

"Just take care of Mishanti, Singe-whiskers."

Fessran grinned back. "Go chase a thistle, clan leader."

Leaving her friend with Mishanti, Ratha paced back along the beach to bring Thakur's request to her daughter.

As Ratha approached Thistle's pool, her steps began to slow. Thistle was not the only one with reasons to deny Thakur's wish. Ratha herself was reluctant to take Thistle along.

Suppose she falls into a fit and goes wild when Thakur is trying to talk to those new clan-cats. Surely he has thought of that problem. Why, then, does he want Thistle to come?

Thistle also had some deep disagreements with the Named about such things as capturing new animals for the clan's herds. What if she decided that face-tails as well as seamares should be left alone? Ratha remembered the trouble Thistle caused when she freed the seamares that the Named had captured.

To her chagrin, Ratha had to admit that Thistle was right about seamares. The web-footed, horselike beasts would never have thrived if the Named had tried to treat them the same as their other herdbeasts. Seamares needed the freedom of the open ocean.

Near the lagoon were several low dunes. Thistle was still in the lagoon. Ratha settled on the crest of the nearest dune, waiting for her to come out.

She watched her daughter glide around the pool with easy strokes of paws and tail. All of the Named could swim if they had to, but Thistle appeared more at home in the water than on land. Ratha had seen Thistle follow the seamares when they plunged into the ocean.

At last Thistle waded out of the lagoon and shook herself. She looked worn, as she often did after such episodes. Hesitantly Ratha came to her and touched noses.

"Fessran still is with Mishanti?" Thistle asked.

"Yes. She can keep him for a while yet."

"Don't want him now. Later. Still shaky."

Thistle settled on her belly in the crusty sand. She slitted her eyes and tucked her forepaws under her chest. Afraid that she might go to sleep, Ratha said hurriedly, "While you were in your pool, Khushi came back with a message from Thakur."

Thistle's milky-green eyes opened wide. "He came back soon?"

"No, he wants us to join him. Both you and me."

"Why?"

Ratha repeated what Khushi had told her.

Thistle turned her nose toward the sea. "Home is here. Seamares are here. Mishanti is here. Thakur knows that."

"I know he does. That he has asked you to come means that it is very important to him."

"Help him talk to other clan-cats? Not clever at talking."

"I don't think that it is cleverness he needs," Ratha said.

"What, then?"

"I don't know. We won't find out until we get there."

Thistle's face took on a stubborn expression. "Hard for me to leave. Thakur knows that," she said again.

Feeling slightly annoyed, Ratha was about to point out how much Thakur had done for Thistle and that she owed him this if nothing else. But she bit back the words. The decision was up to Thistle herself. Trying to sway her would do no good.

"Thakur wants me," Thistle said abruptly. "Do you want me?"

A quick yes would be an easily detected lie. Ratha decided to take the honest but more difficult route. "I can't say that there won't be any problems. Having you along will be difficult in some ways. You know why. All I can say is that I will give you every chance I can." She paused. "I will ask you to do the same for me."

"Can't answer now. Have to talk to sea first," Thistle said.

"The sea?" This was one of her daughter's eccentricities that Ratha had not yet run into.

"I swim out with seamares. Waves break over my ears and tell me things." Thistle got up. Letting her eyes meet Ratha's briefly, she said, "You come here tomorrow. What waves tell me, I will do."

Ratha knew she would have to be content with that. With a quick nose-touch, she parted from her daughter and trotted back along the beach to where Fessran was playing tag with Mishanti.

Fessran halted her game. "What did Thistle say?"

"She has to ask the sea first," Ratha said, a little sourly. She couldn't help letting Fessran know by her tone that she thought Thistle's reply was a bit on the strange side.

"Oh, all she means is that she'll go for a dive with

the seamares and think it over. She has a funny way of putting things sometimes. I find it refreshing."

Ratha sighed as Fessran plunged back into her game with Mishanti.

"Well, I hope the sea tells her what I want to hear," Ratha grumbled to herself, and headed up the trail to get her treeling.

CHAPTER 3

THISTLE WAITED UNTIL Ratha had left the beach. She got up, shook off the sand crusted on her belly, and paced over the dunes toward the seamares' cove. On the way, she passed Fessran, who was still playing tag with Mishanti.

"I'll keep him if you want to nap for a while," Fessran called to her.

"Sleep enough. Swim again. With seamares. Will get Mishanti later."

Fessran waved her tail in agreement. Thistle watched her chase Mishanti. The Firekeeper leader had a reputation for being acerbic and hard to approach, but Thistle found her easier to be with than Ratha.

Perhaps it was because Fessran had also been hurt. She had scars in the sandy fur on her upper foreleg. She had said that someone with very long teeth had bitten her there. There were scars on both the inside and outside of the leg. The teeth had gone right through.

Wonder if teeth hurt her the way Dreambiter hurt me.

From the beach, Thistle crossed onto a series of sandstone ledges beneath the cliffs. She made her way down through the tidepools until she reached the seamares' cove.

There they all were, basking in the sun. Some lay on their bellies with their horselike heads outstretched and their tusks digging into the sand. Others sprawled on their backs or sides, sometimes flipping sand over themselves with a webbed foot.

She lifted her whiskers. She liked seamares. There was something comfortable about their tubby bodies and the way they lumbered and lolled about on land. Their raucous greeting chorus when she walked through the herd and the friendly bumps and swishes she got from their heads and tails made her feel accepted among them.

And she knew a secret about the seamares that nobody else had discovered. On land the creatures were ungainly and clumsy, but in the sea they became beautiful—elegant, streamlined shapes that slipped through the undersea dimness, leaving only a silvery trail of bubbles.

Many creatures of the shore were like that, finding their true beauty in the sea. Perhaps, Thistle mused, she was like that, too. Even though her leg was much better, she could still swim better than she could walk.

She could tell by the dryness of the seamares' velvety fur that they hadn't yet gone on their daily foraging expedition in the ocean. Either she had come at just the right moment or they had waited for her.

Joy surged through Thistle as she trotted into the surf in the midst of the herd of lumbering, hooting seamares. She breasted the incoming swells as they did, then ducked under and swam with powerful strokes of her hind feet. Like the seamares, she used her forelimbs to steer.

Sometimes she wondered if she really was a seamare, somehow born into the wrong body.

The only place she could not follow the herd was down to the ocean floor, where they foraged for shellfish. She had learned that neither her chest nor her ears could withstand the pressure, so while the seamares dove to forage, she remained on the surface. She could act as lookout, spotting any enemies that might come. And at the same time she could think out things that were troubling her.

It was easier for Thistle to think while drifting at the top of the ocean, while being rhythmically lifted and lowered by the swells. Everything seemed clearer out here. The mist that often clouded her mind vanished with the brilliance of the sun on the water.

Thakur had asked her to leave the shore and journey inland. How could she leave the seamares and the ocean? They comforted her, sustained her, renewed her.

It was too much to ask, too much to even think of asking. Away from the sea she became small, ugly, withdrawn into herself. The fits happened more often. The white mist descended on her mind too often, not letting her think.

He knows! Why does he ask?

Yet if he does know, a part of her argued, and he asks anyway, it must be important.

Thistle swam back and forth, trying to find her answer in the ocean's touch. How soothing it felt, washing through her coat, lifting her and rocking her. The others of the Named seldom went into the sea, or, if they did, came out shivering and coughing.

Well, they hadn't grown a heavy undercoat like hers that kept her body's warmth trapped against her skin. And they had never learned to swim the way she did.

Except Thakur. He had let her teach him and he had tried to understand. It was he who had coaxed her out of herself, had helped start the healing in her leg and her mind.

Don't have to help him, even after all he has done. But want to.

And Ratha. Her mother had also asked for her to come. Did that make a difference?

She asked for Thakur's sake. She is not sure herself if she wants me.

Thistle glided and turned as the waves tumbled her gently about. She could feel the sea's muted power. Sometimes it seemed that she could draw more than just comfort from the ocean.

She remembered Ratha's words to her. Her mother had chosen the hard path—the truth. Though stung by those words, Thistle was deeply grateful that Ratha had not tried to conceal her uncertainties.

She asked me to give her a chance. Don't have to, but want to.

When the seamares surfaced, blowing and snorting, she had her answer. Though the journey would be challenging, she would go.

On the following day, Ratha went down to the beach. She had left her own treeling, Ratharee, with Thakur's

Aree, to be cared for by others of the clan. Fessran ambled along beside her.

"Stop fretting, clan leader," the Firekeeper said as they trotted over the rolling dunes, with seabirds crying overhead. "I think Thistle will agree. I wouldn't have come with you to pick up Mishanti if I thought she was going to be stubborn."

"I almost hope that she doesn't want to come. I don't see how she can help Thakur, and I have no idea how I am going to manage her on the trail."

"Manage her?" Fessran howled derisively. "Clan leader, what do you think she is, a herdbeast?"

"All right, she isn't," Ratha snapped, embarrassed. "But I just keep thinking about those fits. . . ."

"They are her worry, not yours. They aren't going to kill her, and if one happens, there are plenty of pools and streams along the way."

Ratha sighed. "I wish you were going, Singe-whiskers."

"Thakur and Bira are already there, and Khushi will travel with you," Fessran said firmly. "We've already agreed on this. I've got enough to do without tagging along to protect you from your daughter."

Ratha was tempted to give Fessran a good swat for that, but the Firekeeper had already sauntered out of reach.

"I'm not afraid of her!" Ratha yowled.

"Not her claws, at any rate. That tongue of hers is sharp enough, even if a little clumsy."

"Bury it, Firekeeper. We're almost there." Ratha picked up her pace, loping ahead of Fessran.

She found Thistle sitting beside her bathing pool,

fluffing her coat in the sun. Ratha and Fessran also sat, waiting for Thistle to dry off.

"What did the sea tell you?" Ratha asked her at last, feeling slightly awkward.

Thistle answered simply. "You and Thakur need me. I will go."

Ratha felt a confusing mixture of delight and dismay at the reply. Glancing at Fessran, she saw the Firekeeper incline her head and lift her whiskers as if to say "I told you so."

Thistle raised her muzzle and gave a high chirping call. Mishanti appeared, covered with wet sand. He had evidently been digging a den.

"When did you start calling him like that?" Fessran asked Thistle.

"Not long ago. He pays better attention to it."

"Good thought. I'll try it out on the little scamp," Fessran said as she swept the cub to her with one paw. "Come on, you son of a seamare. Come with Fessran."

Ratha watched the exchange. She envied Fessran's free and easy manner with Thistle.

Thistle even speaks less awkwardly with Fessran than with me. But as soon as I try to be friendly, she freezes up and I feel bad. I wonder if having her on this trip is really going to work.

As soon as Fessran had gone, carrying Mishanti by the scruff, Ratha turned to Thistle. "Khushi is coming with us. He'll be waiting at the top of the cliff. Are you ready?"

"Yes," Thistle replied softly.

Ratha paced ahead, letting her daughter follow.

* * *

Khushi joined Thistle and her mother on the way up the cliff trail. He would lead, for he knew the way back to Thakur's camp. No more preparation was needed. Thistle knew that Ratha and Khushi had eaten enough to sustain them for several days. She had tried to do the same, although pickings on the beach were a bit sparser than eating from a kill.

"Don't worry about food," Ratha said to Thistle. "I asked you to make this trip, so anything Bira or I catch, we'll share."

Her words were meant as reassurance, but they also reminded Thistle that leaving the beach meant that she was much more vulnerable and dependent on others—something she hated.

As she followed Khushi, with Ratha bringing up the rear, she thought, Perhaps Thakur wants me because he has found others like me. She felt the loneliness rise up inside her along with a strange aching hope. If the other clan-cats Thakur had found were like her, they could understand the paths she had to take, paths that the Named could not follow. Perhaps the strangers could give her as much as she could give them.

CHAPTER 4

It was morning of the third day after they'd set out, and a light rain was falling. The three companions kept to a steady trot. Ratha put Khushi in the lead most of the time. Not only did the young scout know the way, but he chose a pace that was easy for Thistle to keep without straining her nearly healed foreleg. Ratha knew that if she went up front with Khushi, it would be hard for her to keep from leaping ahead, for she was excited and intrigued by Thakur's message.

Another clan like the Named! Could it be? Had Thakur really discovered a group that might band with their own, providing fresh ideas and new talents?

Ratha felt her hopes soar. If Thakur was sure enough to send for her, he must have found another Named clan. His difficulties in speaking with them would quickly be resolved. *They probably have a few different words and customs, that's all.*

Her tail waving in anticipation, she trotted along the trail, eager to speak to the leader of the newly found clan.

★ ★ ★

With Khushi as guide, Thistle and Ratha wound their way over the coastal foothills and then down into a river valley, where the soil was marshy.

Thistle watched as Ratha sniffed some huge round footprints in the damp soil.

She listened as Ratha spoke to Khushi about the footprints. "Face-tails," replied the young scout. "You can't mistake that stink. Almost as bad as Thistle's seamares. We do choose smelly animals, don't we?"

"Well, it makes them easier to find. How far away are Thakur and Bira?" Ratha asked.

"Just up beyond this knoll," Thistle heard the scout reply as he began pacing through the long, waving grass that covered the hill.

Bira met them at the top. Thistle liked the ruddy-coated Firekeeper, with her long plumed tail and gentle manner. Even the acrid smell of the Red Tongue in Bira's coat did not put her off.

Bira had a treeling, a male called Biaree. Thistle was intrigued by treelings. She had never had one and she wasn't sure she wanted one, but they were fun to watch. She saw how they soothed and comforted the Named. Perhaps someday she might like a little companion who could comfort her.

Would a treeling ride on my back when I swim?

Biaree jumped briefly onto Thistle's back for a quick welcoming groom before scampering back to Bira.

"Welcome, everybody," Bira said, touching noses with Ratha and then Khushi. Turning to Thistle, she said, "If you are hungry, I caught some grouse this morning."

Thistle's mouth watered, but first she wanted to see

Thakur. Then she would eat. Bira said she would save the birds. There were plenty for everyone.

Eager to meet her friend again, Thistle scampered after Bira as she trotted down into a little hollow where a campfire burned beneath a sheltering overhang. And there was Thakur, his coppery coat gleaming, his green eyes alight at the sight of her. She was so overjoyed to see him that she broke into a run, dashing ahead of Bira.

"Hello, little seamare herder," Thakur purred, rubbing his chin along her back and flopping his tail over her in greeting.

"Missed you, missed you, missed you," Thistle answered, losing her eloquence to a rush of emotion. "So much, Thakur."

She rubbed her head against him and stood back with a satisfied sigh while the others greeted him and rubbed past him, their tails arching over his back. After the greetings were done, Bira provided the promised repast.

When the meal was finished and the leavings buried, all five relaxed around the small fire and listened to Thakur. As he recounted his experiences with the other cat clan, Thistle listened carefully. He spoke of many things that baffled her. Someone called True-of-voice. Something called "the song." The strange way that the newly found clan seemed to speak and the way that the awareness of an outsider seemed to spread instantaneously through their group.

Thistle also cast glances at Ratha during Thakur's tale. Though her mother's ears stayed up, her whiskers drooped a bit in puzzlement and disappointment.

"These face-tail hunters sound even stranger than I

thought," Ratha said. "Are you sure they are not just another group of the empty-eyed Un-Named?"

"Not completely," Thakur admitted. "But I feel that these clan-cats have the same gift as we do. They just use it differently. Their eyes are not empty, but their awareness is turned . . . inside themselves." Thistle felt his gaze travel to her and rest there as he spoke softly. "As yours was when I first found you."

"Do you think you can bring them outside of themselves, the way you did her?" Ratha asked Thakur.

"Perhaps, although I doubt it. The way they think must be right for them, as our way is for us. I don't think my coaxing will make any of them become like the Named."

Ratha's eyes widened. "Then what do you plan?"

"I tried to speak to them once, but Khushi and I were chased away. I intend to try again. This time I'd like Thistle to come with me."

Thistle's belly began to flutter with anticipation, but she heard a silence as the other four exchanged glances with one another.

"I am afraid that you are venturing on trails where I have trouble following," said Ratha at last. Khushi and Bira made sounds of agreement.

"I know. I'm not comfortable with such things either," said Thakur, and another silence fell.

Thistle ended it. "This song thing. Ears don't hear it?"

Thakur answered, "No. Mine can't. Nor Khushi's. Judging from the way the hunters spoke, they don't listen with their ears. I think they hear it inside their heads. Thistle, you have said things to me that sound as though you can also hear things inside your head."

Thistle felt awkward, though grateful that he had not spoken directly of the Dreambiter. She was not sure how much Khushi or Bira knew about the strange fits that fell on her.

"Yes," she said slowly. "Sometimes I do. Sometimes frightening things, sometimes good things. Not hearing them as much now as I used to. Talking . . . takes them away. When I change the way I think, sometimes they come back."

"Can you still do that? Change the way you think?"

"Not easy. Speaking with you and others—that is easier thing now."

"Would you be able to go back into your old ways if I asked?"

I risk the Dreambiter, Thistle thought, but quickly forced the fear aside.

"Yes," she said, looking straight at him. The look he gave her in return made her feel brave and proud, despite her fear.

Bira asked Thakur a question. "Are you thinking that Thistle can hear the same 'song' as the hunters can? That seems to be expecting a lot."

"Maybe it is," Thakur admitted.

Something made Thistle look at her mother, who was grimacing.

"I must be getting stupid," Ratha growled. "I don't understand any of this. Like trying to pick up water in your paw—it's all running through."

"None of us really understand it," said Thakur. "We're just feeling our way with our whiskers."

And I am, too, thought Thistle, even if I can hear things inside my head.

Ratha got up and stretched. "I may not understand it, but I trust you, Thakur. When do you want to make the attempt?"

"This afternoon. The hunters made a kill this morning. I found it best to approach them after they've eaten and are lazing around."

"All right. I'll hide and watch. I want to see what happens. Both of you be careful," she added as Thistle tried to evade her mother's meaningful glance.

Will try to do what you want. Hard to do things, though. Especially when they are for you.

The Dreambiter was prowling. Thistle felt it as she followed Thakur. The herding teacher was taking her to the new clan-cats he had found—the ones he hoped would be enough like the Named to perhaps form an allied clan. Her mother hoped so, too, perhaps even more than Thakur. Thistle could almost feel the intensity of Ratha's longing and the bleakness of a possible disappointment. Her mother didn't want the Named to be all alone in their world.

The load of hopes was heavy—a hard burden to lay on the back of one who could barely carry her own hopes and griefs, Thistle thought.

Thakur had not asked her to put away her "I-ness," her own sense of identity, but it had fled anyway, swept out by the white mist that now seemed to surround her, containing the small clear area that she walked in and the hard beating of her heart.

He seemed to know what state she was in, and guided her carefully. Down the knoll and into the marshy valley, then up toward the head of the valley, where the wind brought the smell of face-tails and the ones who hunted them.

But Thakur had to tell her all this because the mist was so thick that she could not see very far beyond herself. She could not look over the vast expanse of waving grass and the clear sky she knew was above.

She wondered if she had gone deep enough into the mist. But she knew she could go no deeper, for the Dreambiter was prowling, and if she went in farther, she would meet the terror and fall helplessly on her side.

Should I tell Thakur that the Dreambiter stalks?

No. She could not bear to disappoint him. Or Ratha either.

So she walked inside her own circle in the swirl of white until Thakur's voice told her to stop—they were there.

"Thistle," she heard him say, as if from a distance, "are you ready?"

Her tongue felt strange in her mouth and she had to twist the words from it. "Can't see them, Thakur."

"Over there," he said softly, and his voice was closer, lifting the haze before her eyes. She felt him nudge her muzzle, pointing her head in the right direction. She fought for command of her tongue and voice, for it was that which made the mist thin. With the struggle, the white opacity faded slightly and she saw many cat forms, sitting, lying, or pacing across the open ground.

Thakur's voice was in her ear again. "We will act as though you are one of theirs, lost. I am returning you." He paused. "I may have to back off, since they may remember me. But don't be afraid. I won't leave you. And Bira and Ratha and Khushi are nearby."

Nearby. With the Red Tongue to sear and punish these strangers should they not understand and try to hurt. Their hopes are on . . . me . . . to make the others understand.

Thakur moved forward. She followed. She did as he said and rolled where he told her to. Immersed in the smell of face-tail as well as the swirl of her own confusion, she walked with him to meet the hunters.

In the caverns the Dreambiter prowled.

The cat shapes rose up like shadows in the haze that hung around Thistle. Only the glare of the strangers' eyes gave color to their forms. These were the hunters, the ones whose trail she was to try to follow.

White on gray; the flash of teeth, the red-pink of a tongue. Thakur alongside, his body against her, trying to control his trembling because the other clan knew him from before and he was frightened. She heard the gruffness of their voices, the resolute yet quavering sound of his in reply, giving the tale he had made up.

"Yours . . . lost . . . found and brought back," she heard him say, but he sounded very distant, as if someone had thrown him across the sky.

"That one," came a voice, deep with growling suspicion. Thistle tried to quiet the alarm that went through her. They were speaking about Thakur, not to him. Another voice, its tones harsh, joined the first. "That one with ears that don't work. True-of-voice does not know him."

"A lost one is found," she heard Thakur try again. "In the marshes. Take her back."

The eyes, in all their colors, were turning to Thistle. "A lost one? There are no lost ones if the song is heard."

The eyes were waiting. Thistle felt lost, for there was no song in her head. Nothing but the hollow whisper of a wind through caverns where the Dreambiter stood, no longer prowling, but waiting.

The words were wrapped on her tongue, struggling to come loose. The song is heard, she wanted to say, but the lie could not get free.

And then, deep inside, she heard the echo of something she had never heard before. Not a Named song, not like the sound clan members made, but a thread of something mystical, lyrical. It was without words, yet it had an eloquence that she knew would overwhelm her if she heard its full power.

This was what they called "the song."

She went breathless with the distant beauty of it and longed to rush headlong into the deepest caverns where the source lay. She suddenly wanted, more than anything in the world, to hear the full voice, to bathe herself in it and let it soothe her spirit as the ocean did her body.

A touch on her nose brought her out of herself. It was a male, but not Thakur. The Other One's whiskers brushed hers; his breath went into her mouth; his eyes shone, waiting.

"It is heard," he said, his voice rich, deep, rolling like the swells of the sea.

"The song," she said, knowing that what he meant was that distant, compelling whisper, so faint she feared she might lose it. "So soft, so hard to hear . . ."

The eyes before her seemed puzzled. "Should not be hard to hear. Do what the song says."

She was struggling so hard just to keep hold of the elusive thread that she could have cried aloud with the weight and unfairness of the demand. The song wasn't telling her what to do, except to plunge to the depths of her own being in search of the source.

It was easy to make that headlong dash of the spirit, for something in her was as thirsty for the song as was her throat for fresh water. But another sound, beginning as a hiss and building up to a roar, sent her reeling back. To reach the welling spring of the song, she must meet the Dreambiter.

"No!" she cried, shuddering, dread overwhelming her. Her cry cut the fragile filament of the song, leaving only the wind and the Dreambiter hissing in the caverns.

The Other One knew she was not his kind. The eyes turned away and a growl rose from his throat. Thistle knew she had failed. Sudden agony made her turn and flee, away from the eyes, away from the song, the Dreambiter, and everything.

CHAPTER 5

THAKUR HAD BEEN watching as Thistle's nose met the hunter's muzzle. He had thought for an instant that the other male would attack him, for he clearly had been recognized as an outsider. But the other seemed to have forgotten about him.

He listened. Thistle was speaking, in the same disjointed phrases as the hunter. Her eyes had the same turned-inward look. Was it possible? Could she walk the same trails as these strange, entranced ones?

Thakur admitted he had no real reason to expect that she could. Just a feeling down in his belly. But somehow she was reaching across the boundary, going where he could not, hearing what he could not. . . .

His thoughts were suddenly shattered by a scream from Thistle, a ragged sound that was barely a word.

"No!"

The cry slashed through his hopes, through the slender tie of restraint holding the other clan-cats back from him. Growls and roars exploded from behind him. Instantly he was streaking away beside Thistle, running for his life from the rage of the others who cried out that he was not known to True-of-voice.

Thakur knew that the only thing slowing the hunters was the weight of face-tail meat in their stomachs. Even so, he and Thistle ran far. He could see the strain on her leg, but if he faltered or slowed, they would be overtaken and slain before either Ratha, Khushi, or Bira could catch up and drive the attackers off.

Thistle was limping badly by the time Thakur lost the pursuers. He collapsed together with her in the high grass. The dread that had been making her shudder, even as she ran, now seized her entirely. She went rigid, her eyes blank and glassy.

The spasm tossed her about and then released her, letting her crumple into an exhausted heap of fur. He could not even ask her what had happened, much less tell Khushi, Ratha, and Bira when they galloped up.

"Did the others attack you?" Khushi asked. "I heard Thistle yowl."

Before answering, Thakur nudged Ratha over to lie down by her daughter. When Thistle came out of the unconsciousness that followed her seizures, she needed warmth and comfort. Only when Ratha and Bira were curled about the sleeping Thistle did Thakur say anything about what had happened. Khushi sat to one side, his ears up, his eyes wide.

"It was her cry that started the attack. Before she screamed, I thought everything was going well," Thakur said.

"Then why did she . . . ?" Bira asked softly.

"Something happened . . . inside, I think," Thakur replied. "Bira, maybe what you said is true. I may be asking far too much of her."

Ratha licked Thistle's ruff. "That thing she dreams

about. That's what frightened her. But why did it happen just then?"

"I don't know," Thakur admitted.

"What will you do now?"

"Wait until she recovers and try again."

Ratha fell silent. He watched the expression in her eyes as she stared down at her gifted, troubled daughter.

Thistle had dived very deep in the sea and now she felt herself drifting up. The water was opaque, as if mud had been stirred into it. High above shone a red-orange glow. Not the sun. Another source of illumination. She felt herself rising, turning slowly, moving closer toward the fierce light.

Then, with an odd, sideways motion, as if someone had stuffed her abruptly back into her body, she was in herself again, feeling the warmth of someone beside her, smelling the mingled scents of Thakur and Khushi, Ratha and Bira. Someone else had been lying beside her before she woke. She thought it might have been her mother, but now it was Thakur.

The red light came from a fire-nest that Bira had built and was tending. She saw the Firekeeper move around the flame, feeding it dry wood. The treeling on Bira's back helped, doing with its small hands what the Firekeeper could not accomplish with paws and teeth. On the other side of the flame crouched her mother, fawn coat turned orange by the light, green eyes turning to gold.

Thakur was beside Thistle now and she was glad. He was the one she wanted with her when she came up from those strange sea depths.

He seemed to sense that she had come back, for his voice was low and warm in her ears.

"Thistle?"

She lifted her head, swiveling her ears. Her vision swam and she let her chin drop onto her paws. "Still dizzy," she mumbled, closing her eyes against the firelight. He moved to her other side, blocking out the fire, letting her stare into the cool, soothing velvet of the night. Her mother and Bira were on the far side of the fire. That was good. She wanted them away. What she needed to say now, she could say only to Thakur.

"What made you scream?" he asked softly.

"Wasn't the other clan-cats. Not their fault."

"Could you hear this song they were talking about?"

"Not sure. So faint and far away. Had to go inside. To a scary place. It was there." She faltered, starting to tremble. Thakur knew what "it" was.

"Did your fear of the hunters bring your fit on?" he asked.

"No. Felt strange even before we started. The thing . . . It started prowling. . . . I didn't tell you."

"Why didn't you tell me?" Thakur's voice was faintly reproving, though still gentle.

"Knew you had waited. So long. Wanted to try. For you. Means a lot to you. Didn't want to make you wait . . . anymore."

She heard and felt the depth of his sigh.

"Oh, Thistle . . ."

She snuggled closer to him, felt the warm weight of a paw as he draped it over her. He, more than any of the Named, could accept her for what she was. Yet there was coldness inside her because she had disappointed him.

"All ruined, Thakur? No chance to talk to others?" she asked. "Because of me?"

"Without you we would never have been able to try at all. Next time, though, you must tell me."

"Next time?"

"Yes. If you are willing to try again. If you start feeling strange, though, we will back off and wait."

"Won't they fight us? Chase us away again?"

"I don't know. One time they chased me; another time they let me approach. It is hard to tell what they will do. The only way is to approach them cautiously."

"Want to help you, Thakur," Thistle said. "Will try hard as I can. Maybe next time . . . bad thing . . . will stay away."

Feeling his warmth and his tongue licking the back of her neck, Thistle drifted into sleep.

CHAPTER 6

THREE DAYS LATER, Ratha settled with the other members of her group beside an evening camp-fire. Thistle crouched beside Thakur, her eyes closed, her whiskers drooping. Ratha's heart went out to her daughter. She had watched Thistle try again and again to approach the hunters, only to be attacked and over-come by the prowling terror that lived inside of her.

The thing that wears my shape and uses my teeth, Ratha thought bitterly.

And then Thakur had tried, both alone and with Bira. The face-tail hunters refused. Each encounter was more savage and frightening than the last.

Thakur is going to get himself killed. When I watched from the bushes, I saw nothing to suggest these strangers might be like us. There is no reason to try to talk to them now.

The Named had then changed their tactics, leaving the hunters alone and concentrating on the animals. This hadn't worked either. Any attempt to capture or kill a face-tail sparked retaliation from the other clan. They might not speak, but they certainly thought they owned the face-tail herd, Ratha thought. When the

Named even ventured near, they were met with blind ferocity.

Ratha tried to groom her matted and soot-streaked fur, but gave up. Everybody else looked equally bedraggled and out of sorts.

Too many skirmishes in the last few days had taken much out of them. Ratha could see how her people were starting to suffer. It angered her.

She heard Khushi muttering to Bira as the young Firekeeper and her treeling tended the flame.

"Those hunters are greedy," he growled. "There are plenty of face-tailed beasts for all, yet they keep driving us away."

Bira agreed, her fur ruffled and her usually calm green eyes fiery with indignation. From the corner of her eye, Ratha caught a glimpse of Thakur and Thistle, who had heard Khushi's words. She couldn't help seeing Thakur bristle. Thistle looked tired and defeated. She was also limping slightly—having to run away from the attacks had strained her leg.

Seeing her daughter struggle inflamed Ratha's anger even more.

"I think we have shown enough patience with these hunters," she said. "I heard what Khushi said to Bira and I agree. Trying to speak to them is getting us nowhere."

"I disagree," Thakur said slowly. "Thistle and I did make some progress when we first tried. I understand them a little better than before."

"I don't understand them at all," Bira said, wrinkling her nose. "There is plenty of meat for everyone. Why don't they share? As far as I can see, they are no different than the savage Un-Named."

"Ratha?" The clan leader felt Thakur's gaze go to her.

She answered, trying to control her own impatience. "I sent Khushi here to scout for face-tails. My intent was to add them to our herds. The hunters are making that impossible."

"So you would attack the other clan with the Red Tongue," Thakur said in a low voice.

"Herding teacher, what choice do I have? If we are to survive and grow, we must enlarge our herds. I think these face-tailed beasts can be managed, but we have never really been able to try—the other clan keeps driving us off."

"Perhaps we would be better to look in other places for other animals," Thakur said stubbornly.

Khushi yowled scornfully. "And run away with our tails between our legs if someone else claims them? Herding teacher, I mean no disrespect, but we are the Named, after all. Are we going to back down just because this scruffy bunch is being unreasonable?"

"Enough, Khushi," Ratha said, raising a paw. "Bira? You look like you have something to say."

"Yes, I do," said Bira in her soft voice as she curled her plumed tail around her feet. "I am a Firekeeper. I know how cruel the Red Tongue can be. It is not easy for me to think about using it against others. If I thought these strangers might be like us, I would be horrified by the idea." She paused. "But I have watched them, looking for signs that they are like us. I haven't seen any." She glanced at Thakur and then away again. "Herding teacher, I am sorry."

Despite herself, Ratha was startled. Gentle Bira would give anyone the benefit of the doubt. If even she had hardened her heart, then it must be because the other clan didn't deserve any sympathy.

"What makes you feel that way, Bira?" Thakur asked.

"All the time I have watched this other clan, I have never seen them show any sign of caring for each other—not the way we do. Each one walks past the others as if they were not even there."

"They think differently than we do," Thakur began, but Bira gently, yet firmly, cut him off.

"That should not make a difference. Our treelings think very differently than we do, yet they care for us." She nuzzled her treeling, Biaree, who was snuggled up against her neck.

Thakur had no answer for that. Ratha saw him staring down at the ground between his paws. "I think," he said after a long silence, "that they do care for each other, but in a very different way than we do."

"Herding teacher, is it possible you are seeing something in these people that you only wish was there?" Ratha asked softly.

"I admit I have made that mistake in the past, clan leader. We both have. But this time I think I am right. I only ask for the chance to prove it."

Ratha felt her ears twitch back. "I've given you that chance. I've given the other clan that chance. What can I do if they refuse it?" She sighed. "To be frank with you, Thakur, I don't like these hunters. I like them even less than the witless Un-Named. At least the Un-Named do not enslave themselves willingly to a tyrannical leader, as this True-of-voice seems to be. And they walk around in an endless dream, unable to wake up. It makes me shiver."

"And because you judge them different, you are willing to drive them with the Red Tongue, like animals?" Thakur's voice was very low, nearly a growl.

"My duty is not to the other clan," Ratha snapped. "The Named must come first."

"I thought there might be room in the world for the Named and others as well," Thakur said softly.

"It is their choice whether to attack us," she retorted. "Thakur, the decision is made. We will catch a face-tail tomorrow. If any of the hunters interfere, Bira and I will use the Red Tongue."

She heard Thistle gasp softly, almost a moan of pain, as if she had been struck. For an instant anger burned away the exhaustion in her eyes, and Ratha braced herself to endure a passionate defense of the hunters.

But the spark died, extinguished by weariness. Her daughter only said, "Doesn't matter what Thistle feels. No right to speak anyway. Not clan member." She limped away into the darkness before anyone could stop her.

As much as Ratha wanted to go after her, she knew it would be useless.

She turned instead to Thakur. She thought she had succeeded in becoming hard both inside and outside, but it hurt her to see how Thakur stared at the fire and fell silent.

CHAPTER 7

THE FIRE WAS banked and burning low. Above its crackle Thistle could hear the sounds of breathing—Ratha, Bira, and Khushi were asleep nearby.

Thakur wasn't asleep. Thistle could tell by the way he moved restlessly beside her. She wasn't asleep either, and it was not just his squirming that was keeping her awake.

She was angry at Ratha. Khushi and Bira too, but mostly Ratha. Once again her mother had chosen to strike out at those she did not understand.

She did that to me and she is doing it again to this other clan. I thought she would have learned better by now.

Beside her, Thakur rolled over again, sighed, and started to get up.

"Thakur?" she said, not wanting his comforting warmth to be replaced by the cool night air.

"Sh, Thistle. Don't wake the others. I can't sleep, so I thought I'd go watch the stars for a while."

"Can't sleep either. Go with you?"

"All right, but be quiet."

They left the campfire and the sleepers behind, Thakur

moving noiselessly through the scrub. Thistle glanced back. The fire had become a dim glow in the distance between the trees. When the low boughs and brush overhead opened up to a clear night sky, Thakur sat down and lifted his chin. Thistle did too.

There was no moon that night. Each star was as sharp as the point of a claw. Across part of the sky there was a misty light wafting outward like a plume of smoke from the Red Tongue. To Thistle, the night had a stark, aching beauty.

"It makes me want. . . something I do not even know about," she said, wriggling a little closer to Thakur's warmth.

Thakur said, "It makes me want to lift my paw to the sky, even though I know I cannot reach the stars."

"Night-flying birds," Thistle said. "The mice with wings and big ears—could those creatures fly high enough?"

She felt him give a sigh again. "Somehow . . . I don't think so."

After a long silence, she asked, "Thakur, does . . . she . . . ever sit like this and look up? My mother, I mean."

"I think she did when she was a cub. But that was a long time ago. She hasn't done it for a while."

"Being clan leader is hard. Too many things to think about," Thistle said.

"Too many," Thakur agreed.

Again the silence fell and covered them both. The stars seemed to shimmer against the night sky.

"You were right," said Thistle abruptly. "What you

said—to my mother and the rest—you were right. Don't let anyone make you back away from what you said."

"Why do you say that, Thistle?" Thakur asked in a mild voice. The herding teacher sounded slightly puzzled, as he often did when she took off on a different thought trail without letting him know where she was going.

"Because the other Named ones—they will try to make you say you are wrong about the hunters. And my mother—she will try the hardest of all."

"She is clan leader, Thistle," she heard him say gently. "She is doing what she thinks is best for all of us. She must, or we will not survive."

"Not best for me," she protested. "Not for you either, or for the hunting clan. You said, 'Can't there be room for Named and others as well?' Think there can be." She paused, feeling her whiskers tremble with the force of passion. "Don't let them make you give that up, Thakur."

There was bafflement in the herding teacher's green eyes. "Thistle, what makes you feel so strongly?"

"Don't you think you were right?" she asked, afraid that he was going to change his mind.

"Yes, and I'm glad you think so, too, but I'm just surprised. After all, these hunters have repeatedly attacked us."

Thistle couldn't answer. She wasn't sure. When had this conviction come to her—that the strange clan were more than savage killers? She tried to cast her mind back, remembering. Yes, she had screamed and run away, but she was fleeing from the Dreambiter, not from the strangers. And before that had happened, there was something else, dim and weakly sensed, but powerful.

"They gave me something," she said. "What they call . . . the song." She had looked into a hunter's eyes. She had breathed his breath, touched his whiskers, inhaled his smell. And in all of that was the knowledge of the song; that he heard it and that he knew that she also heard it, however briefly.

She struggled to explain this to Thakur, but the words she found were not the right ones, and her newly made hold on language began to slip.

"Arrr! How can I say it? How?" she blurted in frustration as Thakur tried to soothe her. "Something comes from them. From them into me. And I know that they know . . . Oh, arrr, that isn't right either." Her tail flipped irritably back and forth, but Thakur seemed to have infinite patience.

Finally she said, "I have heard my mother talk about a 'gift' that you Named ones have. That it shows in the eyes. These hunters have something like it, but instead of looking out, they look in. Instead of speaking, they listen. Instead of trying to make sense, they make dreams. Do you understand, Thakur?"

"Only a little."

She stumbled on. "How do I know this? I can't tell you. What they have . . . is like the sea when you swim in it. All around you. Moving into you. Making voices in you. Making you feel the same as when you look up to the sky. The fierce red thing . . ." She fell silent.

"The Red Tongue," Thakur said.

"It would destroy all of that. Wish my mother would understand."

"Perhaps you can help her understand."

"And perhaps you can scratch the stars," she said wryly.

"Thistle . . ."

"Oh, Thakur, how can I lead anyone on this path when I am so lost?" she burst out, feeling an anguish that made her want to cry aloud. She leaned her head against the fur on his breast. He was so gentle, so wise, so eloquent. . . .

She sighed. "Wish I could talk better. But sometimes the words—they run away. Because I am not Named?"

"Thistle, you *are* Named."

"Only through my mother."

"Through your father as well. He was not a clan member, but he had the same gifts. Perhaps he was more gifted than any of us." Thakur paused. "Ratha called him Bonechewer. He was my brother."

Thistle listened to Thakur's heart—strong, steady, and comforting. She had always sensed that he resembled her lost father. Now she knew why.

"If he was what you say, why didn't he pass it to me? Why did my mother think we were all so stupid"—her voice caught—"and drive us away?"

"Thistle, he did pass his gift on to you, but it took a long time to show. I think that is the reason you were slow in growing up. Because you weren't with us, you didn't learn to speak as a cub. That is why you find it difficult now."

"And . . . the driving us away?"

"Ratha told you once," Thakur said softly. "Don't you remember? She couldn't bear the idea that you couldn't be like other Named cubs. But it wasn't your fault, and she told you she was wrong."

"Yes, she did," Thistle admitted. "But it is hard to make her words feel real."

"You may need to hear them again. It may take you many seasons of hearing them."

She let the silence stay for a little while before chasing it away with a question. "I had a brother, didn't I?"

"Two. There were three of you in the litter."

"Are my brothers like me?"

"We don't know, Thistle. We never found them."

"Does my mother . . . want to find them?"

There was a long pause before he answered. "I think you should ask her."

"Maybe I will. But not here. For my mother—too many things to think about."

"Too many," Thakur agreed, yawning. "I feel I can fall asleep now."

Thistle felt her own mouth stretch in a sleepy gape. She followed Thakur back to the campfire and curled up beside him.

CHAPTER 8

IT WAS MORNING. Thistle no longer slept by Thakur. Instead, she had gone away quietly, without waking anyone. Now she crouched, alone in the brush, spying on a band of hunters as they stalked a face-tail. Her mottled coat might be ugly, she thought, but it made her blend in with the background when she didn't want to be seen. She watched, quivering with fright and fascination.

This hunting party was a small group. Its members looked young, some of them perhaps just out of cub-hood. They didn't seem as well organized as the larger hunting band that Thakur had described. Thistle also wondered about their judgment, for they had chosen an older female face-tail with a nursing calf. But perhaps the younger clan-cats did know what they were doing, for they had already managed to separate the pair from the main herd.

A ring of feline hunters now surrounded the beasts. Thistle could see that they were trying to maneuver their prey onto swampy ground, where mother and calf would bog down. But the mother face-tail seemed aware of the danger. Each time two or more of the attackers dashed in to drive her into the trap, the shaggy black-and-brown face-tail gave ground only briefly, then lunged at its tormentors, nearly breaking through their ring.

This is the wrong animal to try for, Thistle thought. This one has been hunted before and knows the tricks.

She watched the young hunters struggle with the wary old face-tail. They seemed unwilling to give up, as if something drove them to try again and again, despite knowing that this creature was the wrong prey.

Even Ratha, for all her stubbornness, would have surely given up by now, Thistle thought. The Named would have recognized they had met their match and chosen another beast.

The old female face-tail was tiring, but so, too, were the hunters. Thistle could see frustration and exhaustion in the rise and fall of their ribs beneath mud-streaked fur. Their feints were becoming slower, and each time one dodged the face-tail's lunges, the tusks came closer.

Why do they keep choosing this animal? I am not a hunter, but even I can see . . .

One of the hunters turned, letting Thistle catch a glimpse of his eyes. Even from the distance, she could see that his gaze was still strangely turned inward, as if he was listening intently, even while he stalked.

"It is the song," Thistle muttered to herself. "It is telling them what to do. And they have to do it."

As she watched, she realized that the hunters had not only chosen an unsuitable animal, but they were trying the same tactics over and over again, even though the beast was wise to them. There was something strangely pitiful and even horrifying about the scene before her, as if the hunters as well as the prey were caught in the trap.

Why was True-of-voice doing this? Thistle wondered. Thought leader cared about people. Or does care, but somehow gets stuck . . . can't understand why hunting didn't work. Can't change.

She knew what would happen almost before it did. The attackers' lunges and feints were slowing, narrowing their escape from the slashing tusks and trampling feet. And then, as one lithe, fawn-colored shadow darted in, the face-tail's great head dipped down, the tusks thrust, and she heard an anguished yowl.

Thistle did not know what seized her legs, making her leap out of the bushes. Or what seized her will either, sending her in to bite and claw at the pillars of the face-tail's rear legs. Looking forward beneath the great shaggy belly, she saw the cat-form of the stricken hunter twist and turn, trying desperately to avoid the huge feet slamming down on the ground.

For an instant Thistle feared the face-tail would ignore her attack, as if she were too small to bother with. It was too intent on the wounded hunter, and even the attacks by the other cats could not turn it away. The bright ribbon of blood on his side was a flag that drew the beast to him. The trampling feet were right above him, and his squall of terror filled the air.

Something whiplike yet heavy struck Thistle's side, sending her tumbling. As she sprang back to her feet she saw that the face-tail had spun away from the wounded hunter and was thundering at her, trunk raised for another blow. She jumped, flattened as it flailed over her back. Her mind was whipping around as fast as the beast's trunk, seeking an escape.

Pure panic made her run for a bluff and sail off the edge. With a bellowing roar, the face-tail came crashing down behind, and she was sure that it would land right on top of her, crushing her. But she landed clear, splashing into a mud puddle.

She shook herself, casting a wary glance at the face-tail, tensing as if she expected the beast to come charging out of the morass beneath the bluff. But the creature was down on its side, thrashing, beating its great trunk against the ground. A fall that was nothing to her had crippled it.

Her fur still on end, she watched the face-tail struggle to rise. The hunters were already appearing on the bluff. She could see their faces, their hunger. The first one leaped down, landing on the heaving mound of the face-tail's body. She heard claws start to rip through woolly hide.

Soon all of the hunters were on the creature, swarming over it as if they had downed it themselves. Thistle felt hungry, but she knew she dared not venture among the horde that was already stripping off the face-tail's flesh.

But one was missing from among them. The young male the face-tail had stabbed with its tusks.

Above the noises of eating, she heard a low moan. It came from up above, where she and the face-tail had gone off the bluff. Her ears flattened.

They leave one of their own to bleed while they feast.

She skirted the great corpse with the hunters tearing

at it. Ears still flat, tail low and twitching, she circled back up to the top of the bluff. Where was the wounded one?

There. Under a bush. A trail of blood on the trampled ground told her he had dragged himself there to die hidden. She halted in midstep, one forefoot lifted. Why should she go to him? There was nothing she could do, and he might just attack her.

It was cruel of them to leave him to suffer while all the others filled their bellies. If he died his life would have paid for that meat. Among the Named that act would have been acknowledged.

Thistle tried to turn aside. Every step that might have taken her away instead brought her closer, until she was within nose-touch of him. Crumpled beneath the low branches of the bush, he looked dead, until she caught the fine tremor of his whiskers and the slight movement of dry leaves before his muzzle that told her he was still breathing.

A shudder went through the wounded hunter. He gasped and cried out like a cub. But there were words in the cry, and Thistle understood them.

"Away . . . from True-of-voice. Dying away . . . alone . . ."

She glanced nervously at the bluff, at the sounds of feasting. Hunters of this same tribe had chased her away. If she had any sense, she would be gone by now. But they seemed engrossed in their prey. She could stay beside the wounded one at least for a little while, offer him warmth and words, if they helped. She knew how it felt to be hurt and alone.

As she crouched down beside the wounded hunter,

his head lifted and his eyes opened. They were a molten gold and seemed to swirl, like water draining inward through a hole.

Inward, thought Thistle. Always inward. These ones dream as they die, dream as they suffer. Aloud she said, "Don't be frightened. I will stay with you as long as I can."

The wounded one's head jerked. The eyes went to her, yet never seemed to fix on her. Thistle wondered if he was blind.

No. All the hunters have eyes like this. Thakur said that I once had eyes like this.

The young male was in a funny half twist that looked uncomfortable. After nudging him to make sure that he had no other injuries besides the tusk wound, she got him arranged so that he was lying on his belly. She had to put herself beside him to prop him up, for he kept wanting to flop over onto his side.

"No," she scolded softly. "Better for you to stay on your belly."

She studied his wound. It was no longer bleeding freely, and it didn't look too bad. There were no bones showing or guts or anything else that should stay inside a body, except blood. But he was trembling and his nose felt cold against hers. The trembling and the coldness. And the fear. The fear could kill, even if the hurt didn't.

She made him keep his head down. Thakur had told her some things about how to take care of the injured. He was a skilled healer. How she wished he were here now!

She looked at her charge critically. On his belly, with his head down, the wounded young male seemed to be doing a bit better. His nose wasn't so cold and his trembling was less violent. Maybe he wouldn't die after all.

"The song," he sighed. "It is heard again. True-of-voice comes to Quiet Hunter."

His words completely baffled her except for his reference to the song. She remembered her own brief experience with it. She had felt from far away the power it had to comfort and soothe.

If the song helped the wounded hunter, she didn't care what it was. She knew she couldn't hear it. She was too far into the self-identified, Named way of thinking. Well, she had to be, in order to look out for herself and for him. She couldn't afford to go stumbling around in a dream-trance. Look what that had gotten him!

The smell of the huge kill made her belly growl. He must be hungry, too, since he was stalking with them. With disgust she noted that none of those now feasting on the downed face-tail had even glanced around for their injured companion.

Thistle remembered what Bira had said at the campfire. She was reluctant to admit that she would agree with one of the Named, but Bira was right. These people seemed to feel no compassion for one another. They could plan and carry out an elaborate hunt, but they were not capable of the feelings that she and the Named both shared.

How could I have thought that they are like us?

This wounded male—he was the same. Even if he lived, he would never be able to look at her with eyes that understood what she was. She had nothing in common with him or his people. She had no business being there at all. She should go.

CHAPTER 9

THISTLE WAS GIVING the wounded male a soft farewell nudge when movement at the corner of her vision made her glance up. One of the hunters, a large, heavy-shouldered male, was climbing a trail up the side of the bluff. He had come from the kill. He had a chunk of meat in his jaws.

Thistle was sure that he would eat it himself, that he would walk right past the two of them. Instead he paced deliberately to the bush where the wounded male lay. Unsure whether to freeze or run, Thistle stayed where she was. The large male ignored her, laid the meat down before his injured clan-mate. . . .

An excited shiver went down Thistle's back, all the way along her tail.

Bira is wrong! These hunters do care about each other.

Stretching out his neck, the injured male got the tips of his fangs into the meat and dragged it to him. The intoxicating food smell washed over Thistle, forcing her to fight an impulse to snatch some. Instead she crouched slightly apart from the injured male, watching.

When he had eaten, others of his kind brought more.

They also gave him small melons from a vine that grew nearby. Thistle had seen the Named eat these to slake thirst when there was no good water.

Those who brought the meat and melons gazed briefly at her. Their eyes were distant, but Thistle had no doubt they saw her and recognized her. Why didn't they chase her away?

Perhaps they know that I tried to help.

Her belly rumbled again and she swallowed. Would they mind if she had just a little of the meat and melon? She crept toward the nearest piece, sniffed it, and almost jumped out of her pelt when the wounded male pushed it toward her with his nose.

Thinking that the others might not approve of his act, she glanced at them, tensing to flee if anyone showed raised hackles. But no one did. Soon she was gulping face-tail meat and crunching moist melon, enjoying its juicy coolness on her tongue.

Once the wounded male had eaten, he rested and then tried to groom himself. The bleeding from his tusk wound had dwindled to a slow seepage, but Thistle feared that if he twisted around to lick himself, he might start bleeding again.

"Don't try," she said softly. "Will do it for you."

He looked faintly baffled at her words but seemed to understand her intent. He lay quietly as she worked on him, using her teeth and raspy tongue to clean the fur around the wound. Several of the hunters gathered around, as if to watch, although their odd, dreamy gaze made Thistle feel as though they were looking right through her.

She was startled when one spoke. The voice was light,

female. "True-of-voice has learned of the hurt done to Quiet Hunter."

Thistle, unsure whether the speaker was talking to her or not, glanced at her companion. He was washing his face, but he paused, put his paw down, and lay, eyes closed, ears forward as if listening.

"True-of-voice sings healing," said someone else.

Thistle itched with curiosity. Who was this True-of-voice? A clan leader, like her mother, Ratha? She realized that she didn't know if the unknown singer was male or female. He or she might even be right here, watching. Thistle had no way to tell.

These people . . . so strange. Know why Thakur could not talk to them.

She felt lost and uneasy. What if this True-of-voice found out about her, realized that she was an outsider, ordered the others to attack her?

In her uncertainty she had moved close to the wounded male and was now huddling against him.

"The song's healing is for all." She both heard and felt her companion's voice as it vibrated through his body.

If you can hear it, she thought, her ears twitching crossly. Did hear it once. Had to go deep inside myself.

Dare she try that again? It would leave her open, vulnerable, dream-entranced.

But they are all like that, too.

She glanced around at the cat shapes surrounding her. Their eyes never met hers and they avoided her gaze as if it was too sharp, too direct. She felt left out, as if everyone were speaking a silent language she could not understand.

Her only choice was to go . . . inside.

Again she pushed away her feeling of identity, of self. There was no one named Thistle-chaser. There was no one with a name. There was nobody and no names. . . .

And she, without self, without name, walked in mist-shrouded caverns, following a haunting, distant call. It had a voice, but no words. It did not need speech. The rise and fall of the voice itself spoke with an eloquence beyond words. It drew her like the scent of one beloved, and she realized that it was not just a sound but a scent as well—distant, tenuous, yet powerful just as the voice was. It resonated not only in her senses, but in her whole being.

The desire in her grew frantic. Her longing to find the singer, to feel surrounded by the strength and sureness of the song, hurtled her headlong through the depths of herself.

There were no questions in the song. There were no doubts. The voice, the smell, the feeling, all promised an end to uncertainty. She would not need to seek. The singer, the song . . . already knew.

That was why the singer was called True-of-voice.

To one who walked so much on the edge, to one for whom the questions overwhelmed the answers, the song was a lure that could not be escaped. It was the sound in her ears, the intoxicating scent in her nose, the feeling in her skin as if someone she loved was rubbing against her. It was everything she wanted and had never thought she could have.

And she could plunge down the trails of herself forever in search of it. . . .

Until a growling roar shattered the distant music, and her skin prickled and burned.

She had forgotten the guardian of the caverns. Her mind's eye, seeking the beautiful shape of the singer, flinched away from the apparition of the Dreambiter.

She tried to turn back, but the nightmare was on her, fiery with hate, teeth sinking deep into her shoulder and chest. She sought the outside, the self, the name, but the Dreambiter had her. She knew that it would keep her until it had exacted the price of her daring.

Thistle fled, both within and without, the blackness sweeping over her even as she ran. It took her from the wounded male she had tried to help, from those who had been watching, from the song, and, worst of all, from the unknown singer called True-of-voice.

She might have hurt someone in her panic, even the injured male she had been tending. As her shaking legs gave way and she felt herself begin the slow topple onto her side, she gave one last cry for forgiveness.

The young male lay by himself on the grass. He had been hurt in the fight by the face-tail's tusks. The song and his clan-mates called him Quiet Hunter, but he did not identify himself by that name or any other.

The body that moved, the legs that walked, the mouth that ate, the flank that had bled, the tongue that spoke— they were all gathered together in a vague way that the mind recognized only dimly.

When another clan mate spoke the words *Quiet Hunter*, the young male acted or answered, but that was all. He said words that could bring a response from others—Kinked Tail, Bent Whiskers, Nose-to-one-side, and, of course, True-of-voice.

Those words were only used to make a clan-mate say or do something. They were spoken when he wanted something from the others. Except for True-of-voice. There was never any need to ask anything of True-of-voice. The source of the song always knew what was needed.

Except when Quiet Hunter was first stabbed by the face-tail's tusks in the fight. True-of-voice was too far away then. Terror and cold had made the song fade. The fading brought fear. Fear that there would be a great silence.

The fur on the young male's brow wrinkled. Somebody else had come. Not True-of-voice, though True-of-voice had helped later. The first helper was an outsider, not a clan mate. A female. Gentle, kind. With words that helped to chase away emptiness and coax the song back. Yet the song did not know her. How could this be? The song did not know her, yet allowed her to stay. The song never accepted those not known to True-of-voice.

The female had made everything better. Now he could eat, groom, and even stretch a bit without harming the wound. The gash was scabbing over. The belly could feel full after eating, and Quiet Hunter could lie in the midnight dark and let the song bring comfort.

There was gladness that the song allowed the female to stay. She made the feelings better. Yet she was . . . disturbing. Her ears didn't work; she barely heard True-of-voice. Or so her words said. How could she be so deaf to the song, yet still live?

Perhaps that was why she did strange things. Hopping around on three legs. Saying words that meant nothing. Running away.

She needed to hear the song. There was something inside her that hurt. Even more than a tusk wound.

And the young male that the song knew as Quiet Hunter lay thinking about how strange the world was.

CHAPTER 10

THAKUR STIRRED IN his sleep. The warm spot that Thistle made against his back had grown cold. Blinking, he lifted his head, thinking that she had just shifted to one side. No. She was gone.

Sleep fled as he jumped to his feet. Ratha, curled up against Bira with her nose buried in her tail, was startled awake.

"What . . . ? Arrr! Where's Thistle?"

"What we talked about last night upset her," Thakur said. "No, you stay here," he added as Ratha started to get up. "I know where she went."

"Oh, no! She's trying to talk to the face-tail hunters again." Ratha groaned. "Thakur, she'll get herself shredded by that bunch."

"They'll shred you if you start running out into their midst. I have some experience with them. You wait. I'll find out what happened to Thistle."

Before Ratha had a chance to object, he galloped away into the scrub forest. Soon he reached the open land where the face-tail hunters stalked their quarry. From a distance he saw the exposed bones of their kill at the foot of a small bluff. When he climbed the trail to the top of the bluff and hid in the brush nearby, his gaze turned toward the group of cat figures there. Among them he spotted a familiar mottled red-brown and orange coat.

Thistle's head was down. She was eating. They were sharing food with her! How . . . ?

Thakur stayed hidden downwind from the group, not wanting to interfere. He stared at the scene, filled with amazement. Somehow Thistle had done what he could not. The other clan had accepted her. An injured young male lay near her. From the look of his wound, he had been gored by a face-tail. Had she been tending him?

Yet something odd was happening in the group. Everyone was sitting, staring at nothing. Even Thistle.

Thakur crept closer, intensely curious. Things were changing. Thistle looked frightened. Arrr! She was starting to jump around in circles on three legs, the way she did when she went into one of her fits.

Not now, Thistle! he wanted to yowl. He knew it would be useless. She couldn't control what was happening.

Fearing that the others would attack, he tensed, ready to rush in and defend her. They didn't, although some backed away from her, looking puzzled. As Thistle broke into a panicked run, they moved aside for her.

Silently Thakur stole through the brush and the high grass, trying to guess where her crazy zigzag path would take her. At last he was far enough away from the hunters so that he didn't worry about being scented or seen. He bounded toward Thistle and intercepted her.

She staggered, fell on her side, and began to thrash. Eyes wide open, but blank, she struggled, trying to

speak. "Wanted to help . . . but couldn't . . . ran inside
. . . to hear . . . song for healing. . . . Why . . . does
he hear it when I can't. . . ."

"Thistle, don't try," Thakur said.

"He . . . knows how much . . . it hurts. . . . Didn't
want to run from them. . . . Afraid, couldn't help . . .
Will hate me . . . Dreambiter . . ." She shook violently.

Thakur lay down alongside Thistle, draping his paws
and tail over her. The warmth and the weight seemed
to help, for she closed her eyes and her limbs became
still. He thought that she would fall into a deep sleep,
but instead she spoke again.

"I could have reached them," she hissed, her voice
raw. "If I hadn't let . . . the badness . . . have me. . . ."

"You can go back," Thakur said, trying to soothe
her. "You can try again, Thistle."

"No. . . . They saw the badness. . . . Afraid of me
now. . . . Jumped around, clawed somebody . . . hurt
them. . . . No trust . . . anymore. . . ."

"You didn't hurt anyone. There is nothing to be
ashamed of," Thakur soothed.

"Should fight the badness, not run . . . away. . . ."
Thistle's voice slowed and slid as exhaustion took her.
Thakur could feel the wiry little body go limp beneath
him.

Gently he pulled his paws out from around her. She
would feel nothing for a while.

Why is it so hard for her? he asked silently, and found
himself hackling, as if there were a flesh-and-blood enemy that he could fight for her sake.

He sighed, made his fur lie flat, and licked Thistle's

cheek. He had to think what to do next. She had managed to reach the hunters and get accepted. But she had ruined that tentative bond, or so she thought. What would happen if and when she tried again? The answer lies with that wounded young male. She was caring for him. Perhaps they will allow her back.

He grimaced. There were too many questions, uncertainties, fears. Besides, Ratha and Bira were coming, and he had no idea how to explain what had happened. He decided that he wasn't even going to try.

"Come with me. Please," Thistle said to Thakur above the soft crackle of the fire. It was afternoon, but Ratha had Bira light one just in case the hunters had followed.

Thakur tried to quiet Thistle. He was attempting to listen to Ratha, who was talking to Bira and Khushi about how they might capture a young face-tail. It was hard, because he was sitting away from them in order to tend Thistle. Ratha had been helping him while Thistle was still groggy, but when her eyes and mind cleared, Ratha had retreated to the other side of the fire.

He turned back to Thistle when she tried to get up and wobbled.

"Face-tail hunters. Need to . . ."

"You've done all you can," Thakur said, trying to soothe her.

"No. Need to show you something. Important."

All his cajoling could not make her lie down again. With a sigh, he told the others that he and Thistle were going for a short walk and would soon be back.

Her eyes seemed to light from inside, as if they were

seawater with the sun pouring through. Despite her shakiness, she bounded ahead. Thakur had to trot to catch up.

"What do you need to show me?" he asked, drawing abreast of her.

"Can't say. Can only see."

She led him to a place where they could observe the face-tail hunters without being sighted or smelled. "Watch," she said, once they were settled.

"What am I looking for?" he asked mildly.

"Remember what Bira said—about hunters not caring for each other?" Thistle turned her head, her eyes large with excitement. "The wounded one. I helped him. There he is. Watch others near him."

Puzzled, he did as she asked. The wounded male still lay alone, although he seemed to be better. The others went about their business, evidently ignoring him.

"Help him," said Thistle under her breath, as if she were speaking to them.

"Thistle, I don't think they will. . . ."

"Did before. Was there."

"Yes, but things were different because you were there. They might have copied you. And maybe he doesn't need help any longer."

"Have to help him," said Thistle, her voice intense. "To show *you*."

Thakur allowed himself one tail-twitch of annoyance and then relaxed. It would do no good to say that the hunters didn't know that he and Thistle were there and so would not do anything to "show" their observers.

He was starting to announce that it was about time

to return to the others when Thistle went stiff. "Look," she hissed. "Look *now*."

The wounded male was no longer alone. A party of the hunters surrounded him. Two were grooming him while several others were bringing meat from the face-tail carcass and melons from the patch that grew nearby.

Thakur watched carefully to be sure that he wasn't seeing what he wanted to see. But it was hard to mistake the intent of those who were nursing their injured clan mate. They cared. They understood pain and answered with compassion.

"Didn't learn it from me," Thistle said in a low voice.

"You are right, Thistle," Thakur said, feeling excitement growing in him.

"That big one. Gray with white belly. Coming toward them. Think he is True-of-voice."

Thakur studied the distant shape. It was definitely male, huge and heavy-shouldered, with a ruff. Deep gold eyes stared out of a wide gray face streaked with black.

"Why do you think he is True-of-voice?" he asked Thistle softly.

"Song said he was. Before, when I heard it. . . . Hard to explain, Thakur."

If the figure was not True-of-voice, he was some sort of leader, for everyone drew aside and crouched out of his way. Was it because they feared him?

Thakur remembered the tyrant, Shongshar, who had forced Ratha out of the clan and then ruled it heartlessly. Ratha had had to kill him to free the Named and win back her leadership. Was this True-of-voice another of the same breed?

Perhaps. But the hunters also seemed to need him. At their call, he came and touched noses with each of them. Each one stretched his or her neck forward eagerly, as if the brief nose-touch was a food more nourishing than meat or a drink more thirst-quenching than water.

Thakur thought that the gray-and-white leader would approach the wounded male and groom him, but instead he sat down close by. The others formed a loose circle around the injured hunter and the large male Thistle called True-of-voice.

"True-of-voice singing to wounded one," said Thistle, with an odd catch in her own voice. Was it longing? Thakur wondered. Did she want to be out there in the circle, "hearing," in some strange way, a soothing voice that helped and comforted?

"Need more than food or water to heal." It was Thistle again, speaking softly.

How do you know these things, Thistle? Thakur wanted to ask, but instead he said, "I think Ratha should see this."

"Bring her," Thistle said, her eyes never leaving the other clan. She seemed to be drawn to them—an attraction that made Thakur wary.

"You come back with me," he said.

"No. Stay here. *Need* to stay here."

"I'm afraid you won't stay hidden. You'll try to join them."

"Want to," Thistle admitted. "Now not good, though. Will stay, Thakur. Bring my mother."

Nothing could sway Thistle when she was being stubborn. But she knew that it would not be an advantageous time to approach the hunters. She might disrupt whatever was going on between the gray-and-white leader and the wounded young hunter. And there was definitely something going on. Thakur could almost feel it.

Quickly he padded away to fetch Ratha.

Sometime later the clan leader of the Named crouched beside Thakur in a bush that hid them from view. Thistle had obeyed him and had stayed still, even though he knew she had been tempted to join the other clan.

"Wounded hunter and True-of-voice still there," Thistle said as Ratha settled beside Thakur. "Others too."

"So that is the one you call True-of-voice," Ratha hissed after she had been watching awhile. "He's got a good set of teeth."

Thakur could tell by the look in Thistle's eyes that she wanted to tell her mother about the strange "song" that was healing the injured hunter. But Ratha's first comments had not encouraged her.

The scene with the wounded male and his leader went on for a long time. At last the circle around the two broke up, and its members wandered off to groom or nap.

"See?" Thistle said triumphantly to Ratha. "You and Bira—wrong, wrong, wrong! Hunters do take care of hurt ones!"

Ratha sent an annoyed look toward her, and Thakur groaned inwardly. Neither mother nor daughter was gifted with much in the way of tact.

"All right, I do see it," Ratha said after a long silence. "Are you sure that the ones feeding the young male aren't just his parents?"

"Too old to treat like cub," Thistle said scornfully.

Thakur agreed.

"Bringing food to True-of-voice, too," Thistle added. "He didn't ask them."

Thakur glanced at Ratha, who was studying the scene with narrowed eyes.

"They don't need to fawn all over him," she muttered. "All right, I admit I have made a misjudgment. These hunters obviously do share some of our ways. If they would stop driving us away from the face-tails, maybe we could reach some sort of agreement."

"Have you seen enough?" Thakur asked her.

"Yes. Let's go back. I want to think."

CHAPTER 11

At the fire where the Named gathered, Ratha crouched with Bira, Khushi, and Thakur, listening to her daughter speak. Thistle was talking about her experiences with the face-tail hunters and how she had learned more about them.

When Thakur had returned that previous morning, with Thistle at his side, Ratha had been too grateful to ask questions, even though Thistle was subdued and looked as if she had been through another fit. She seemed to have recovered, but listening to her now, Ratha couldn't help wondering. What she said seemed so nebulous and strange. And she actually seemed comfortable with the nature of the face-tail hunters!

Every word she says about them makes me shiver inside. How can she think that understanding more about this clan will make me accept them?

Ratha tried to keep her nose from wrinkling and her tail from twitching, but she found it hard to hide her repugnance. Thakur evidently spotted her reaction, for after Thistle had finished speaking and curled up near the fire to rest, the herding teacher approached Ratha and took her aside.

"Clan leader, come with me," he said, and they walked away from the fire together.

"I hope you are not taking me to watch that hunting bunch again," Ratha said crossly when they were away from the others.

The herding teacher looked at her quizzically. "You really don't like them, do you?"

"It is worse than that. Thakur, I hate them. I wish they were all gone, or dead." She surprised herself with the coldness in her voice.

Thakur's silence told her more eloquently than any words the depth of his shock and surprise.

"You never thought you would hear such things from me, did you?" she said wryly, but her whiskers trembled.

"No."

She stopped, facing him. "You want to know why those hunters make my belly crawl? It's that leader of theirs, that True-of-voice character. From what I saw and what Thistle said, he sounds worse than any of the Un-Named, or even Shongshar. Shongshar may have been a tyrant, but he couldn't take away anyone's thoughts. This True-of-voice seems to have something slimy oozing out of him that turns his people into infant cubs."

"Thistle didn't use those kinds of words," Thakur said.

"Thistle was so befuddled she couldn't see the truth. How would you like having someone talking in your ear all the time so that you couldn't think for yourself?"

"I wouldn't," Thakur confessed.

"Well then?"

"Ratha, just because such a thing is wrong for you or me doesn't mean that it is wrong for the face-tail hunters."

"How can anything be wrong or right if you don't even have a choice?" she countered.

"All right. The way these hunters are controlled is hard to accept. I'm not having an easy time either."

"I can't even think about accepting it. I can't believe anyone would want to stumble around in a trance their whole life. If this True-of-voice really forces his will on his people, he is bad," Ratha said bluntly, and added, "Maybe the best thing we could do for them is to kill him."

She watched Thakur's green eyes go wide, and his teeth flashed as he spoke. "You don't know enough to judge," he said, his voice hard.

"There are times when I've known even less about an enemy, yet I've acted. How much did I know about the Un-Named when I first used fire against them?"

"Do you have to think of these hunters as enemies? When you saw them, you said they share some of our ways."

"Yes. I also saw how well they worked together and how devoted they are to their leader. They are a threat. I can't pretend that I'm blind to it. We need to show our strength by wielding the Red Tongue." She looked away from Thakur, then back. "I'm doing what I did when the Un-Named attacked us. It worked. And I never heard you speak out against it."

"Perhaps I should have spoken out against it," Thakur said in a voice that was nearly a growl. "Or maybe I should have spoken louder. Clan leader, we of the

Named have already learned that things are not as simple as we once thought. We can no longer divide the world of creatures into those who are like us and those who are not."

"It is easier to do that when you are clan leader," Ratha said, feeling both shamed and justified. "Thakur, you know that I have to choose in favor of our people."

"Does something that helps the Named have to hurt others?"

The green in his eyes seemed to burn into her, making her tongue clumsy. "N-no. But somehow it has happened that way."

"In past seasons we were struggling so hard to survive that we couldn't afford to worry about who we hurt. But now—and I credit your leadership, Ratha—things are better. We are not so much on the edge. Maybe we can afford to be more understanding. It may have unexpected rewards."

Ratha eyed him. "You are thinking about Thistle, aren't you?"

"Yes."

She switched her tail. "Sometimes I wish you didn't think so much, herding teacher. You'd be easier to live with."

"I probably would be," Thakur agreed.

"So you want me to postpone any face-tail hunts. How long?"

"Long enough for Thistle and me to convince you that True-of-voice's people are not enemies."

Ratha sighed. "All right. I'll delay the hunt I'd planned and I'll explain why to Bira and Khushi. If I have any rash impulses to go shred True-of-voice, I'll sit on them."

"Or talk to me about them," Thakur suggested.

She grimaced. "I don't think that even you can make me feel differently about True-of-voice. My belly really doesn't like him. I'm being patient for your sake, not his."

"I appreciate that you are being patient. The reason doesn't matter."

And I'm doing this for your sake too, Thistle, Ratha thought as she jogged back to the campfire beside Thakur.

CHAPTER 12

FOR THE THIRD time in less than a day, Thakur watched Thistle's eyes begin to swirl as her body went rigid and started to tremble.

He felt his own heart pound in his chest. He hated seeing this happen to her. He hated it even more when there were others around to witness her helplessness. Luckily, this time, no one was. He had taken her to a little hollow where they could be alone, where she could practice slipping into the dreaming state of mind that was so like that of the hunters.

Instead she was battling a nightmare.

"Come out of it, Thistle," Thakur yowled as her pupils shrank to black slits in the stormy green sea of her eyes. "You've had enough. *I've* had enough."

Twice before she had managed to pull herself out of the trance before it took her. But this time she was gone where only she could go.

Thakur had chosen this place for another reason. It had a pool. A marshy little wallow of a pool that was more mud than water.

She was starting to jump around, muttering nervously to herself. Thakur grabbed her by the scruff before she could dash off on a mad run, and swung her with a splash into the pool.

"There," he said. "Now come back to me."

Her pupils expanded with surprise as she started to thrash in the pool. The water was colder here than in the beach lagoon where she swam. He grabbed her scruff again until he felt her relax.

"Thistle?"

"Y-y-yes?"

She was shivering. He hauled her out and made her shake dry, then spread himself beside her to warm her up.

"Bad again," she said, looking disconsolately at the ground between her paws. "Every time I go . . . inside . . . it . . . is there."

Thakur didn't have to ask what "it" was. He groomed the nape of her neck with his tongue.

"Have to try again," she said stubbornly.

"Not today," he answered.

"Yes, today. Have to talk to hunters."

Thakur groaned. "Thistle, you're tired."

"Know. Talking getting not easy. Words running and hiding."

"Then give it up for now."

Thistle closed her eyes and let her head sink onto her paws. "Give it up for now," she muttered. "Try and fail again tomorrow too? Can't. Others. Him. The hurt one. Means too much."

"Sh," he said softly.

"Can't . . . sleep . . . have to . . . talk. . . ." But by the time the last word had fallen from her tongue, she was deep in slumber.

* * *

The next day was a repeat of the first. The following was the same. Thakur spent all his waking time with Thistle as she sought the pathways inside herself and was driven out by the apparition she called the Dreambiter.

Thakur had lost count of how many times he had watched the sea-green in her eyes swallow her pupils as she struggled in the grip of each fit. He also lost count of how many times he had thrown her into the pool and hauled her out. It was the only way to keep the seizures from claiming her completely.

His legs and belly were encrusted with mud. He was starting to sneeze from the repeated chill. His teeth ached and his mood had soured.

Thistle lay in a sodden puddle on the ground. She was so exhausted after the last attempt that she hadn't even been able to shake off before collapsing. Thakur was almost glad that she was unconscious again. It meant that she couldn't try to brave the Dreambiter.

He ran a paw along her side, trying to squeeze the muddy water out of her coat. At least the sun was warm today. It would dry her quickly.

He stared at her funny pointed little face, the eyes now shut, muddy smears on her nose and whiskers. His heart ached for her. Why is it so hard? Why does this wretched Dreambiter have to bar her way?

He watched the water dry on her coat, feeling helpless. This is beyond her. It is beyond me. Perhaps it is beyond all of us.

"Thakur?" said a voice. He lifted his head and stared at—the Dreambiter? His fur bristled before he could flatten it. Then he shook himself. It was just Ratha. Yarr! He was getting so involved in Thistle's struggle that sometimes he felt as though he, too, could see the nightmare image. It took a shape he knew well.

Ratha crouched by Thistle, gave her a tentative nudge.

"Don't worry, she won't wake up. After that last fit, she's going to be out for a while. You can show her a little affection if you like. She won't feel it."

Ratha shot him such a hurt look that he instantly regretted the words.

"I'm sorry," he said curtly. "Three days of struggling with this hasn't helped my patience. I shouldn't take it out on you."

Ratha put a paw on her daughter and tried to squeeze more water out of her fur. "She's a mess. You're a mess. What are you attempting to do?"

"I thought I explained it." Thakur, trying to groom himself, sneezed into his fur.

"Here, sit down and let me clean you up," Ratha said. She spat and grimaced after her first lick. "Ugh. That mud tastes awful."

"I know," Thakur answered.

"So she's trying to get herself into that sleepwalking state to talk to the hunters?" she asked. "Is it working?"

"No. Every time she tries, something kicks off another one of her fits."

"Something?"

"The Dreambiter."

He saw Ratha shift her gaze, felt an angry twist in his stomach. She was going to back off again, retreat into her clan-leader role. She's leaving me with the responsibility that should be hers.

"You don't like to hear that word, do you?" Thakur said, his voice flat.

Ratha yanked a piece of dried clay from his belly. It took some fur with it. She spat it out, then backed away. "I think I'll come back when you are in a better mood."

"Are you going to run away again, clan leader?"

"Thakur, I don't know what kind of burr you've got in your coat this time, but—"

"I don't have a burr. I've got your daughter. *Your* daughter," he said again. "And I'm fed up with seeing you run away from her."

He watched Ratha's eyes narrow. "I gave you what you asked for. I gave you both a chance to talk to the hunters."

"Yes, you did. I need more than that, Ratha. I need your help."

He could almost see her closing down inside, becoming remote. "There is nothing I can do," she said. "If Thistle can't overcome this . . ."

"She can't. Not alone. Not with me either. She needs you."

"Why? I can't do anything for her. She doesn't need a mother. She's responsible for herself."

"I want you to face your part in her life," Thakur snapped. "Who is the Dreambiter, Ratha?"

Again she looked away, and when she looked back, her green eyes were blazing. "Don't blame that on me, herding teacher. That thing isn't me. It's part of her sickness. She dreamed it up. Why, I don't know. But she made it."

"Yes, she made it," Thakur said, his voice steady. "It looks like you."

Ratha flinched. "I bit her when she was a cub. I know I did. I was impatient. I wanted her to talk, to be like other Named cubs. I couldn't accept that she wasn't. I can't go back and undo everything." He heard her voice start to tremble. "It is all in the past. You can't change the past."

"For Thistle it is not the past. Ratha, I am not trying to blame you. I am only saying that both of you created the Dreambiter. It will take both of you to put it to rest."

A sudden look came over Ratha's face, one Thakur had never seen before. He found himself staring at her in fascination and frustration. He had seen her triumphant, angry, grieving, even scared. But never had he witnessed this expression of utter dread that seemed to steal the life from her face and drain the color from her eyes.

Her voice sank to a whisper. "I can't, Thakur. I've given you what I can. A chance. I can't give any more."

She was backing, turning tail. A part of her had already fled far away.

"Ratha, please don't run," he said softly.

She glanced back at him, a glance so filled with torment that it seemed to hit him like a blow.

"Tell her I was here," she said, and before Thakur could speak or move, she was gone.

CHAPTER 13

With Bira and Khushi, Ratha made her way along the outskirts of the face-tail herd. The animals spread over the river plain, and there were some small groups that had broken off from the main herd.

It was the morning of the day following her talk with Thakur. She wasn't ready to face him again. Nor did she want to see Thistle.

"Surely the hunters won't bother us here," said Bira, when the three found several face-tails and their young in a small side valley between two hills.

"We've just come to watch the animals," Khushi reminded her. "Ratha said that we need to learn more before we try to catch one again."

The clan leader listened to them, feeling slightly guilty. She wasn't going to break her promise to Thakur, but he had said nothing about scouting the beasts. Well, watching was all they would do, no matter how the creatures tempted her. Anyhow, Thakur wasn't with them and he was the best at dealing with face-tails.

He was also the only one who could cope effectively with Thistle. He had said he would keep her from trying again to make herself ready to talk with the hunters. There was no reason to, at least for now.

No sooner had she, Bira, and Khushi settled down in the grass to watch the face-tails than Bira's sharp eyes caught movement in a bush nearby.

"That is definitely *not* a face-tail," Bira said. "I think the hunters are spying on us."

Ratha considered a hasty retreat, but the idea made her hackles rise. Khushi and Bira both agreed with her. They weren't going to be frightened off by one spy.

"They don't own the whole face-tail herd," Khushi said indignantly.

"Perhaps the watcher will just stay hidden and report later," the more even-tempered Bira suggested. "But I could go and light a torch from the fire-den I dug."

"No," Ratha said. She wanted to keep her promise to Thakur. She had disappointed him—and Thistle—in so many ways already. She wasn't going to add another, although Bira's offer was tempting. She would like to feed these arrogant hunters a small taste of the Red Tongue.

She turned her attention to watching the face-tails, but it was hard to keep her mind on the big animals.

Maybe Thakur is right. Maybe we should just move on and leave these animals to the hunters. Then we could forget about them, and Thakur wouldn't need me to help him with Thistle.

"The spy just left," said Bira, who had been keeping an eye on the suspicious bush. "I think he's gone to get the others."

"Let them come," growled Khushi.

As much as Ratha shared his feelings, she realized that they were at a big disadvantage. And without the Red Tongue . . .

Bira wanted to bring a torch. I should have let her. But I promised Thakur.

"No," she said again. "We're going back to the fire-den. I doubt if they will follow us there, but just in case . . ."

Quickly she got the two others moving through the long grass. Having to retreat stuck in her throat, and she could tell by the looks on the others' faces that it stuck in theirs, too.

We are the Named. We shouldn't let ourselves be chased off by a bunch of sleepwalking hunters. I almost hope they do chase us to the fire-den so we can feed them the Red Tongue!

Khushi, scouting briefly from the top of a hill, reported that the spy from the hunters had indeed gone to fetch some reinforcements. However, they seemed to be content just to make sure the Named had left the face-tail herd.

"We could make another try at a different place in the herd," he suggested when he got back.

"No, they'll find us and chase us off again," Ratha said, disgusted.

"How can they watch the whole herd?" Bira wondered.

"I don't know. They seem to be very well organized." Ratha paused, her tail twitching with annoyance. "I think we're going to have to make a choice. The only way we are going to get near those face-tails is by using the Red Tongue to scare off the hunters."

"I think we should," Khushi argued. "I'm fed up with playing hide-in-the-grass."

"But you said that you made a promise to Thakur not to," Bira said gently to Ratha, coming alongside her.

"I may have to rethink it. I will talk to him when we get back."

As Ratha paced toward the camp with the others, she argued with herself.

Most of the Named would say I am justified in using the Red Tongue against True-of-voice and his bunch. We used it against the Un-Named in order to survive. This is the same situation.

She shook herself as she ran. She didn't need justification. Her rage was enough. True-of-voice was a filthy tyrant and his subjects mindless fools. The world would be better without them. She should set the Red Tongue against them, burn them out.

She drew her lips back from her fangs as she imagined the grass afire on the plain, the hunters and their prey fleeing in terror, or falling, exhausted, and burning to death in the flames.

And then, suddenly, one of those frightened shapes fleeing from the fire in her mind was her daughter. The flames caught up with Thistle, surrounded her, consumed her, leaving her body black and charred. . . .

No! Ratha recoiled from the imagined scene in horror. Not Thistle. Why was she thinking like this?

"Clan leader? Are you . . . all right?"

The voice beside her was Bira's. Ratha realized that she had slowed to a stop and was staring straight ahead at nothing.

"I'm all right," she said, her voice feeling rough in her throat. "Bira, Khushi, go on ahead. I'll follow."

Both of them gave her a backward glance as they left. Then she was alone. She checked briefly for any sign of enemies or ambush before she went on slowly, immersed once more in her thoughts.

Again she seemed to look upon the fire-swept ground where the hunters had once been. It was swept clean of them.

Instead of triumph, she felt only horror.

Not only because her daughter had been among those seared by the fire's touch. The high, waving grass was burned to stubble. The blue sky had gone gray. The whole landscape before her was ashen, hellish with cruelty and the terrible knowledge of what she had done in the name of survival.

Ratha closed her eyes, bent her head in pain. No, no, no . . . I would never . . . But she knew that a part of her would.

There was something in her that was as ruthless and relentless as the Red Tongue itself, that burned with hatred and consumed those around her.

There were many who had felt its searing touch. The old clan leader, who had died with a flaming brand jammed through his lower jaw. Thakur's brother Bonechewer. The Un-Named ones who had fallen in the first battle with fire as a weapon. The cubs she had borne in the litter that included Thistle. The usurper Shongshar, whom she had thrown down in a bitter fight that had nearly cost the life of her friend Fessran. Thistle, who had known the terrible shock and pain of her own mother's teeth sinking deep into her chest and foreleg.

She had nearly destroyed the Named themselves and she had certainly changed them.

And now the victims would include True-of-voice and his people.

Thistle had a name for the fiery wildness that struck out, not caring who it hurt: the Dreambiter.

The Dreambiter.

No, I am not. . . . She made it. . . . I am not. . . .

In the midst of her denial, she heard Thakur's voice, speaking in her memory.

Ratha, don't run.

Don't run from your daughter. Don't run from yourself.

How can I not run? This part of me hurts, kills, hates. . . . The Dreambiter. It consumes everything. Soon it will swallow the rest of me.

No. Ratha clamped her jaws together. I don't have to let it take over. I can fight it. I *will* fight it. I will drive it out of my daughter's life and out of mine.

Yet it was hard to take those steps along the trail that would lead her back to Thakur; hard to say, Yes, I will help you with Thistle.

She stopped, caught in indecision. The hatred was still there. She still hated the hunters, wanted to burn them. She still dreaded the Dreambiter and dreaded even more the look on Thakur's face when he realized that she really *was* the Dreambiter.

Thakur, I don't want you to turn away from me.

Please don't hate me, despite what I am, despite what I've done. . . .

She forced herself to take a step, even though her legs felt as though they were sheathed in ice. She shut down all the thoughts in her mind except one as she walked stiffly back toward the camp.

I have to kill the Dreambiter.

CHAPTER 14

THAKUR LOOKED DUMBFOUNDED when Ratha stood before him and said the words that she had been practicing all the way along the trail.

"You've changed your mind?" he said. "You'll work with Thistle and me?"

"Yes. Anything to help her get rid of this nightmare."

Thakur gave her an odd look, and she realized that she had spoken as if the nightmare were also hers. Well, it was.

"Do you mind if I ask you why?"

"Because of what you said to me. I have been running away. Now I'm ready to fight."

Thakur gave her another strange look, but he seemed to be satisfied. After all, it was he who was asking for her help, not the other way around. Or was it?

Quietly he led her to Thistle, who was having a nap by the dunking pond. Ratha could see that her daughter had obeyed Thakur by not attempting to go into any trances and thus risk the apparition again. Instead, she had rested, and eaten to gain strength. She looked good, her coat better groomed and dry.

When Thistle woke up and saw that Ratha had joined them, she looked a little nervous.

"Must have been hard deciding," she said, glancing shyly at her mother.

"Yes."

"Hope you don't mind . . . getting wet. Thakur throws me in pond. . . . Chases the . . ." She faltered, then went on. "Chases the bad away."

"Perhaps I won't have to do that anymore," Thakur said, with a glance at the pond. "Thistle, Ratha, are you ready?"

Thistle sat up straighter, her whiskers bristling. Ratha realized that she couldn't tell which of her daughter's forelegs had been the crippled one. She seemed to use both equally well now.

"I'm ready, although I don't know exactly what to do," Ratha said.

In answer, Thakur lay down, forming himself into a half circle around Thistle, his tail lying across hers, his head lifted so that he could look into her eyes. You make the rest of the circle, his eyes seemed to tell Ratha. She arranged herself on the other side of Thistle, draping her tail across Thakur's and bringing up her forepaws to touch his. Her belly lay against her daughter's rear foot and flank.

"All right, Thistle. Go . . . inside," Thakur said.

The clear green in Thistle's eyes seemed to shift, as if a cloud were moving across sunlit water. Her breathing grew fast and shallow and her jaw opened as she panted.

Thakur's voice was soft yet strong. "Don't be afraid. We're here. We're both here."

Thistle swallowed, but her panting eased. Ratha's own heart was pounding so hard she thought that Thakur might be able to hear it. Mingled dread and excitement swept through her. At last she was going to meet and battle the enemy.

"Dreaming," Thistle said in a distant voice. "Caves. Walking. Speaking not easy."

"Say what you can," Thakur coaxed.

"Oh!" Thistle gave a sharp indrawn breath.

"What?" Ratha asked, her voice tight with anxiety and eagerness.

"Easy, Ratha," Thakur said softly, pushing his forefeet against hers.

"Even here. Far away. It comes."

"The badness?" Thakur asked.

"Oh, no!" Thistle's face was rapt. "Good. Sweet. Want to follow."

Thakur looked surprised. "The song? You can hear True-of-voice's song?"

"Yes. So faint. Want to be closer."

Thakur leaned closer to Ratha, who was bursting with impatience. "She's picking up the song, the thing True-of-voice sends out to his people. I'm surprised. They're pretty far away from us."

"It won't hurt her, will it? It won't take her over?" Ratha's worry made her whisper harsh. She felt intensely uncomfortable with the idea that the strange leader of the hunters could somehow reach from a distance and lure her daughter. She had thought she would have to fight only one threat. Not two.

"Want to go closer," Thistle begged.

"Go," Thakur answered.

A look crept across Thistle's face that Ratha had rarely, if ever, seen. It was happiness. Pure delight.

"Not walking anymore," Thistle said. "Swimming. Like . . . in the sea. But warmer. Softer." Again she gave a sharp gasp. "Oh! Ahead brightness, shape, color, beauty . . . sweetness in the ears, the nose, the eyes, the skin, everywhere. No words good enough to say."

"To say what, Thistle?" Thakur asked gently.

"What it is. What he is. What she is."

"True-of-voice?"

"More than True-of-voice. Wise ones sing through him. Wise ones now dead sing through him. Fathers, mothers, all sing through him."

Ratha felt her fur prickle as she listened. Wonder and dread fought inside her. This was stranger than anything she had ever encountered before. And it was in her own daughter! What was Thistle-chaser? More than Named. More than Un-Named. Something else, working through both, had shaped her.

"I'm lost, Thistle," Ratha heard Thakur say.

"Not lost. Never be lost again." Her daughter's voice was breathy. The black of her pupils had gone to tiny slits in swirls of sea-green.

"I mean that I don't understand."

"Will tell you. When I come back."

Come back! She might never come back. Ratha gave Thakur's forefoot a sharp push to get his attention. "Where's she going? What is this?"

"I don't know. She's never gone this far before," Thakur admitted. "Having you here has done something."

"It's scaring me. Take her out of it."

"It's not frightening her. Let her go, Ratha. She knows this path better than you."

"I don't want to lose her! Seeing her sitting there, staring at nothing, makes me feel as though I have a million fleas in my fur. She might . . . just . . . stay . . . like that for the rest of her life."

Thakur started to say something, but Thistle interrupted. Her voice was strangely light and she turned her head to gaze at Ratha, although the remoteness was still in her eyes.

"Do not be afraid, my mother. Can come back if I want. Help me to go on. Need you to help me go on."

"Thistle, I care too much. I'm frightened. This is too strange. Come back. Please. I—I love you."

"Must reach where the hunters are to speak to them."

"I-is it that important to you?"

"Yes. If you give love, give trust too."

Ratha closed her eyes, pressed her feet against Thakur's, feeling the answering warmth. "Then I trust you. Go where you must."

"Not sure about doing. But must try."

Ratha opened her eyes, fixing her gaze on her daughter as Thistle continued her inward flight. Who had given her this ability? The one called Bonechewer who was her father, the brash and gifted outsider, Thakur's brother?

Or was the ability from Ratha's own lineage, a trait that had hidden among her parents and grandparents to emerge now in her daughter?

"Where are you now, Thistle?" Ratha asked, feeling her voice trembling.

"Swimming, but no closer. Sea is getting thick, heavy. Brightness ahead hard to see. Something . . . coming between."

Ratha tensed.

Thistle's voice rose in pitch. "Down deep. Getting cold. Swimming too hard. Have to walk. In the distance, hear footsteps."

This was it. The long-dreaded enemy was at last making an approach. Ratha saw Thakur squirm closer to Thistle, guarding her, protecting her.

What good will it do when the enemy is inside? Ratha thought in despair, but she also wriggled closer to Thistle.

"Can't block the way!" Thistle cried out in sudden rage. "Fight you, fire-eyes. Tear you before you can tear me!"

She sank to a crouch, her forepaws sliding out in front of her. She was starting to shake. Ratha could feel it.

And then Thistle began to draw one foot up against her chest, as if the leg that had been healed was being crippled again, right before Ratha's eyes.

"No, you aren't going to take her again!" Ratha cried, as if the nightmare could hear her. "Fight it, Thistle. Drive it off!"

But Thistle only seemed to crumple under a terrible weight of pain, her leg pulled tightly against her chest. Ratha felt a storm of rage building inside her against the thing that tortured her daughter.

In her mind she flung herself at the enemy, ripped it with her claws, savaged it with her teeth, and then set it aflame with a torch. In a low, hissing voice, she spoke her battle aloud, and the depth of her hatred. She would kill the Dreambiter a thousand times if she had to, rip out its throat and its guts so that it bled.

But it was Thistle who bled. From an invisible wound. And each time Ratha screamed her rage at the Dreambiter, Thistle drew a little further into a tight ball of pain.

And at last, though Ratha was far from emptied of rage, the sight, the feel, the smell of her daughter's suffering made her voice break as she cried, "Thistle, I am with you. I hate this thing as much as you do. Fight it . . . Please fight it."

But Thistle only huddled and shuddered. Thakur put a paw on Ratha's nose to quiet her. She jerked her head back, baring her teeth, the wildness and the anger focusing on him, wanting to attack him.

Everything was fierce, wild, flaming. She would hurt, she would kill if she did not get away. It was out of control. She had to run or the fire inside her would destroy Thakur, Thistle, everything.

She was already on her feet, running, not caring where she went. She would charge into the midst of the hunters and go down in a last frenzied battle. She would tear her way through them until she found True-of-voice and locked her teeth in his throat.

And then something heavy landed on her back, squashing her flat. Rage, astonishment, and fear combined in a murderous frenzy and she squirmed wildly, trying to get at her assailant with claws and teeth.

But somehow he managed to pin her down and grab her scruff, pulling her head so far back that all she could do was claw the air. She spat, screeched, and struggled until her throat was raw and she was panting with exhaustion.

"Enough, Ratha?" said a muffled voice above and behind her head.

Hearing Thakur sent her into another wild flurry, but she was too spent to sustain it.

"Can I let your scruff go, or will I get shredded?"

"You'll get shredded," she growled, but she was too tired to make the threat real. Thakur released his grip, but stayed on her back.

"Go to Thistle," Ratha growled.

"Bira's looking after her. Am I too heavy?"

"Go to Thistle!" she yowled, trying to throw him off. "She's the one who deserves you. She's the one who's hurt."

"Is she the only one, Ratha?"

His soft voice, his warm weight, the very strength of his presence seemed to enfold her. Yet somehow it could not penetrate the hard center of misery deep in her chest.

"You can heal," she gasped. "You can help. All I can do is . . . hate."

Instead of saying anything, he began licking the fur on her neck.

"Don't, Thakur," she said, starting to shake.

"Why not?"

"If you knew what I really am, you wouldn't."

She felt his tongue caress her nape again. "I know what you are."

"The Dreambiter. That's what I am," she said bitterly. "I hate the Dreambiter. I want to kill the Dreambiter . . . yet I am the Dreambiter."

"Ratha," Thakur began.

"I think that finding the Red Tongue poisoned me. All I can do is hurt and burn. The Red Tongue is in me. It is getting stronger. Soon it will take the whole of me. It will be all hate and biting and burning."

"Not all, Ratha."

"Keep sitting on me, Thakur. I want to rip everything to pieces and I will, if you let me go." She struggled again, but was almost thankful when he kept her down. "That's good. Keep sitting on the Dreambiter. Maybe a quick bite to the throat will get rid of her for good."

"That is only another way to escape."

"Let me escape, then. Why do you want me? Why would you keep something so dangerous in your midst?"

"Ratha, we are all dangerous. To ourselves and each other. Not just because we have claws and teeth. The Un-Named have those as well. Not even because we have the Red Tongue."

"Then . . . why?" Ratha whimpered.

"Because we can hurt and be hurt in new and deeper ways. We are all Dreambiters. And Dreambitten as well."

"If that is so, we should all be dead. Maybe the world was never meant for the Named. Or the Named for the world."

"I don't think so, Ratha. And you don't either. You were the one who fought hardest of all to see us live."

"Maybe I was wrong. If all we can do is birth cubs who have to struggle, like Thistle . . ."

"And you," Thakur added softly.

"All right, maybe me," she said grudgingly. "What

difference does it make? It doesn't help Thistle. I can't
do anything to help Thistle. That's what drives me so
wild. I can't go near her. I'm afraid I'll hurt her. Thakur,
maybe I'm going to have to go away. . . ."

"No. If you choose escape, no matter what way, she
will always have the Dreambiter."

"But if all I can do is hate the Dreambiter and that
doesn't work, what else is there?"

"I think you have to remember who the Dreambiter
is," said Thakur.

Feeling the bleakness in her belly, she said, "I *know*
who it is."

"No, you don't."

She craned her head around and stared at him, lost.

"You think that it's all of you. It is only a part of
you. And not even the strongest part."

"No," she cried, despairing. "You say that because
you think I am like you. I'm not, Thakur. You are
patient and wise and good and caring. I'm not."

"Well, I'll admit you aren't very patient and you are
still learning. But you do care."

"The Dreambiter doesn't care. The Dreambiter just
. . . bites."

"You are like me, Ratha. And because I know you
are like me, I can say this. We all have a part that bites.
Even me. You've seen it. You saw it just a while ago.
But the other part, the part you call good and caring,
is stronger."

"In you, maybe," Ratha muttered.

"No, in you. You have it. It won't let the Dreambiter
take over."

Ratha was silent, taking long breaths.

"You have it," Thakur said again. "Trust in it."

Somehow his words made her tight knot of misery ease. "Maybe . . . ," she said in a low voice.

"Maybe what?"

"Maybe you can get off me now. I don't feel so much like ripping up things."

He eased himself off and let her groom her rumpled fur. "See? I trust your better self," he said. "You should, too."

"Just for that, I should give you a swipe across the nose," Ratha said, shaking herself. "But you're bigger than I am. Is that what you call my better part?"

"Somewhat. It's also your common sense."

Ratha paused. "I need to think. Hard."

"Do you want me to leave you alone for a while?"

"No, I want you to stay. Don't say anything. Just sit by me."

And Thakur did.

CHAPTER 15

"YOU WILL GUIDE me?" Thistle stared at Ratha. The doubt in her eyes made Ratha want to squirm. Or change the decision she had made after thinking a long time. "You, not Thakur?"

"He will help," Ratha said, "but this time it has to be me."

Thistle looked away.

"Please, Thistle. I think I understand more now."

"About you or me?"

"Both," said Ratha.

"Then lie down around me," Thistle answered, her voice trembling with a strange mixture of fear and anticipation.

Ratha could not watch her daughter withdraw into herself. Instead she fixed her gaze on Thakur. He pressed one of his forefeet against hers in silent support.

She waited, and at last it came—she heard the footsteps of the Dreambiter, echoing in Thistle's voice. Again Ratha found herself bristling with anger against the unseen enemy, but she knew now that rage could not drive off the apparition.

She knew that for Thistle, she existed in two parts: the flesh-and-blood mother with a tawny coat and an uncertain temperament, and the fire-eyed punisher that lurked in the caverns to ambush the wandering self. She was both and neither.

As she wriggled close to her daughter, she could feel Thistle's pounding heartbeat shaking her small frame. Thakur, on the other side, moved closer, too, helping to encase Thistle in a shield of warm fur and life. Yet the deadly thing—the deathly thing—was inside, beyond reach.

Tell Thistle to flee? To fight? Ratha suddenly didn't know. Her decision, her plans—all somehow crumbled when faced with the small figure who trembled and whose foreleg was starting to draw up against her chest.

"Where are you, Thistle?"

"In the caves. Hearing the footsteps. Want to run."

"No," Ratha said. "Stay."

"Wait for attack." Thistle's voice was leaden with the inevitability of pain.

Hearing it, Ratha rebelled. She would not let the drama end as it had already a hundred times before. But she had no plan. Just the feelings that twisted her belly and a stubbornness that refused to let her daughter suffer more.

"No," Ratha said, and then added softly, "Call the Dreambiter."

"Call . . . But then it comes faster. Pain . . . sooner . . ."

"Call it," Ratha said again. "Call . . . her."

"Too frightened. Don't want it." Thistle's voice was starting to become high and panicky.

"What happens when the Dreambiter comes?" Ratha asked gently.

"Hurts. Has to hurt."

"What if it didn't hurt?"

"Has to hurt. Is what Dreambiter is for. Has to hurt. If not me, then . . ."

"Then what, Thistle?"

"Then . . . others."

"Who?"

"Mishanti. Thakur. Fessran." Thistle paused. "You," she whispered in a tight voice.

"If the Dreambiter is inside, how can it come out and hurt others?" Ratha asked.

"Takes my claws, my teeth. My . . . cleverness too. Could kill," Thistle added.

The cold flatness of her voice made Ratha shiver. The implied threat was not empty. Ratha remembered her struggle with a maddened Thistle-chaser on the wave-washed rocks. Her daughter had come frighteningly close to killing her.

Thistle moaned, and the green swirling in her eyes expanded. "It . . . coming." Her limbs started to jerk and twitch as if she were trying to run away.

"Call to the Dreambiter," Ratha urged, following an impulse she didn't understand.

"Coming anyway; why call?"

"Call it to you. Call . . . her."

"Might come out . . . try to hurt."

Ratha suppressed a shiver. "Call her anyway."

Thistle closed her eyes, lifted her muzzle, spoke in a quaver. "Dreambiter, come. Tired of waiting, tired of fearing."

"Good. More," Ratha coaxed.

"Come to me, fire-eyes. No more hiding. Biting . . . not the worst part."

"What is the worst part, Thistle?"

"Knowing who you are, Dreambiter."

The answer startled Ratha. For an instant she thought her daughter was deliberately provoking her, then she realized that she had somehow become the apparition's voice. Again she rebelled, angered and grieved that Thistle could not get beyond that image. But this time she refused to give in to the anger.

Knowing who you are. Wandering alone in the caverns, fire blazing in my eyes. Oh, how I wanted to love you when you were young, Thistle, but I thought you would never speak, would never know me, would never be able to love in the way the Named do.

"Call me, Thistle," she whispered, her throat dry.

"Call hurting part? Part that would bite and burn?"

"Call me," Ratha said. "And tame me."

"Can't."

"Yes, you can. Tell me you are not afraid. Tell me you are stronger than I am."

Thistle had been starting to crumple again, curling inward. Now she shoved both forepaws ahead of her, as if propping herself up.

"Am stronger than you, Dreambiter."

"You won't let me out. You won't let me hurt."

"No. Come, Dreambiter."

"I am coming," Ratha said softly, watching Thistle. She could almost imagine herself in the shape and form of the dream image, pacing through the caverns toward a distant shape.

I want . . . so much. That is why it hurts.

Come to me, terrifying one, beloved one. I hear Thistle call. Come even if you rend me. You are a part of
me even as I am of you. One flesh, one lineage . . . one
pain.

The Dreambiter hurts, too.

"I need you," Thistle said.

"I am coming. But I do not know what I will do
when I reach you."

In a dreamy but intense voice, Thistle spoke, her face
rapt. "See you now. Your coat . . . black, eyes orange.
You . . . more powerful than ever but now you are
beautiful. You leap. . . ."

Thistle broke off with a gasp and a violent jerk. Ratha
feared she was going into one of her fits, but she seemed
to recover herself and went on.

"Leaped right at me as if . . . going to attack. Landed
on me, but did not weigh me down. Instead . . . soaking
into me . . . like drop of water falling on my coat."

Thistle shook her head. She had lost the entranced
look and had come outside herself. And she stared at
Ratha in perplexity.

"What happened?" Ratha asked.

"Not know, exactly. Except that it . . . wasn't bad.
Was afraid, then . . . everything changed."

"You didn't go into a fit this time. Does that mean
that the Dreambiter is . . . gone?" Ratha asked hope-
fully.

"No, not gone," Thistle said, looking thoughtful.
"But somehow . . . changed." Her jaws gaped in a sudden yawn.

"Well, I think we've gotten somewhere," said Thakur. "I'm not sure exactly where, but perhaps things will sort themselves out." He got up, stretched until his tail quivered.

"So sleepy," Thistle mumbled. "Don't know why."

Ratha nudged Thistle so that her drooping head lay against Ratha's belly. The rest of her curled up in the circle of Ratha's limbs, and soon her sides began rising and falling in a long, regular rhythm.

"I was going to ask you if you wanted to take a walk, clan leader," Thakur said, "but I guess you won't be able to."

"No," said Ratha, gazing down at the sleeping Thistle and thinking of what she had looked like as a nursling. "I won't be able to go. But I don't mind. Even if she snores a little. Isn't that funny?"

"Dreambiters can be comfortable to sleep on," said Thakur, and walked off, swinging his tail.

Ratha was surprised when Thakur told her later the same day that Thistle's struggles with the Dreambiter were far from ended. Yes, they had made a beginning, and a good one, but nightmares that had been building for a lifetime would not be banished by a single healing encounter.

She began to see the truth of his warning that evening as she watched Thistle make her strange inward journeys, her eyes lit by firelight, seeking a trancelike state that would let her "speak" to the hunters and hear their guiding song.

Sometimes the inward path was clear; more often the Dreambiter lurked and Thistle had to fight her way past. The only evidence of the struggle was the language of

Thistle's body and the words she spoke. At times her speech was more eloquent than Ratha thought her capable of. At other times the words were so broken and tumbled that even Thakur, with all his patience and insight, could make little of them.

Yet something had changed. No longer was Thistle a helpless victim, fleeing from the apparition every time it struck. Now the contest was more even, and an attempted trance did not have to end in a fit.

Even so, Ratha did not expect to hear Thistle say that she was ready to try again to speak to the hunters. It was the following evening, and the Named crouched around the fire that Bira tended.

"It has only been two days," Ratha said, startled herself at how short the time had been. To try to talk to the hunters before the Dreambiter had been completely mastered seemed to be inviting disaster. "I know I am the impatient one," she admitted. "But maybe it would be better to give yourself a few more days, Thistle."

"Won't help," Thistle said bluntly. "Have gone as far as possible alone or with you and Thakur. Need the hunters. Before they and the face-tailed animals go away."

"Go away?" Ratha asked, puzzled.

"Sense a stirring. Hunters and prey. Moving. Long ways."

"How do you know?"

"Feel it. In the song."

"I think she's right, Ratha," said Thakur, who was lying on the other side of her. He looked to Khushi. "You've been keeping watch on the face-tail herd.

Didn't you tell me that the beasts might be preparing to migrate?"

"Yes. They seem restless," the scout replied.

"Hunters will follow," Thistle added.

"You are sure that it is not just the hunters who plan to go?" Ratha said, thinking that if the other group would disappear and leave the face-tail herd, the Named could take an animal without interference.

"Would be happy thing for you if hunters just went away," Thistle said, a little bitterly. "No. Both will go. Soon. Need to speak before then."

"All right." Ratha sighed. "When?"

"Morning. Tomorrow."

"Thakur?" Ratha looked to the herding teacher.

"Thistle thinks she is ready. I agree," he said softly.

"Will you be going with her? Or do you want me?"

"Neither." It was Thistle who answered, not Thakur.

Immediately Ratha began to bristle. "Now wait. No one said anything about you going by yourself."

"Have to," Thistle replied calmly. "You and Thakur can't think like hunters. Get chased away. Not me. Did it once before," she added, with a trace of smugness that irritated Ratha.

"Yes, you did. And if I'd known about it, I would have stopped you. It was just luck that you didn't get killed the first time."

"Not luck," retorted Thistle. "Quiet Hunter. Helped him. They knew."

"Thakur," Ratha began, appealing to the herding teacher, but he only put his nose down on his paws, pointing toward Thistle.

She stared again at her daughter, wondering how that scrawny, scruffy-coated little body could contain such a determined spirit.

She knows full well that she doesn't have to obey me since she isn't a member of the clan.

"Will be careful," Thistle said. "Don't want to get hurt."

"All right," Ratha said at last. "But Bira and I are going to back you up with torches. We'll stay out of sight, but if anything happens, you get your tail out of there and let us handle the fighting."

"Won't be fighting," Thistle said, sounding exasperated. She turned her intense gaze on Ratha, and the words she had spoken earlier seemed to sound again in Ratha's mind. If you love, give trust too.

The problem is, Ratha thought as she studied the expression on that stubborn little face, can I trust *them*?

CHAPTER 16

THISTLE WRINKLED HER nose as she stood by Thakur in the shelter of some low brush. Her mother and the Firekeeper Bira had insisted on bringing the smoke-breathing thing they called the Red Tongue. Luckily the wind was blowing the acrid scent away from the plain where the face-tails grazed.

The hunters had taken and feasted on another animal. The meat smell was heavy in the wind.

"There," said Thakur quietly, staring toward a lone male who was walking stiffly across the open grass. "That's Quiet Hunter, isn't it?"

Thistle looked eagerly in the same direction. She liked Quiet Hunter and had missed him, perhaps more than she'd realized. She wanted to bound out to meet him, but decided that a cautious approach was probably better.

Glancing back she saw Bira tending a small fire in a cleared area while Khushi laid out sticks to serve as torches if the need arose. Ratha was overseeing the preparations.

Thistle took in the scene with mixed feelings. It was good that her mother and the others wanted to protect her. But they could ruin everything if they ran out into the midst of Quiet Hunter's people with torches.

"Make sure . . . fire carriers stay here," she said to Thakur. "Don't want them . . . unless fighting happens. And it shouldn't."

He promised that he would, and Thistle left the sheltering thicket and walked toward Quiet Hunter.

Her heart felt as though it were slamming around inside her ribs, like a trapped creature seeking a way out. Would the others accept her again? Or would they remember that she had behaved strangely the first time, falling into a fit and then fleeing. Would Quiet Hunter remember that she had cared for him, tried to heal him? Or would he sense her difference and turn on her, or worse yet, summon the others to drive her away?

As she approached the young male, she saw others take notice. Heads turned and muzzles pointed in her direction, but no one rose to challenge. Without turning his gaze toward her, Quiet Hunter seemed to know she was there. He stopped walking and stood still, as if waiting.

Almost shyly, she came up and touched noses with him. The coolness of his nose leather, the brush of his whiskers, the scent of his fur seemed to draw Thistle inward, away from her outside self. She did not have to initiate the journey into trance. It just seemed to happen.

She knew an instant of fear, for she sensed that she was back in the depths where the Dreambiter prowled. But something coming from Quiet Hunter seemed to hold the apparition away, letting her move forward on the path toward a distant voice and a haunting song.

At last he spoke to her. "There is rejoicing. One who gave care and healing has come back."

An upsurge of affection made Thistle rub her head against his, words spilling from her. "Didn't want to run away. Fond of Quiet Hunter. Wanted to stay and help. Got afraid. Of things inside."

"Things inside can frighten and hurt most of all," said Quiet Hunter. "But the song heals. Quiet Hunter likes . . ." He faltered, puzzled. "The words that belong. They are not known."

"Thistle-chaser," she said, knowing that in his strange way, he was asking for her name. "Easier to say just Thistle."

"Quiet Hunter likes Thistle," he answered, his eyes glowing.

"And Thistle likes Quiet Hunter," she said, rubbing herself alongside him, her eyes closed in happiness. When she opened them again, she was startled to see that others had come up and were standing in a circle around her and Quiet Hunter.

Again she felt a flash of panic and the distant thread of the song was interrupted by the echoing roar of the Dreambiter.

"Do not be afraid," said Quiet Hunter. "All know of the help and the healing. All wish to touch noses and share the song. Bent Whiskers wishes to be first."

Hesitantly Thistle turned to the old female whose kinked whiskers had earned her the name. She brought her muzzle up to the other's, breathed her scent. And as she did, she thought the song that was singing deep inside grew stronger.

Next was Tooth-broke-on-a-bone. As Thistle touched his nose and breathed his scent, the song increased again, not only in power, but in clarity and beauty.

With each greeting, each recognition, the strength of the internal melody grew, but never became unbearable. Thistle's spirit leaped in wild joy. Quiet Hunter and his people were her brothers and sisters. These ones knew her in a way that the Named never could. And they had a gift that all of the cleverness and eloquence of the Named could not equal—a wordless acceptance that wrapped her in warmth and lifted her spirit to dizzying heights.

The song soared within her, joining her with those who also heard and were seized by its power. Fright, doubt, uncertainty were all swept away by the golden voice.

Nearly breathless with awe and joy, she turned to the last of those in the circle. Quiet Hunter did not have to say the words that belonged to this one. Thistle already knew who he was.

True-of-voice.

Trembling, she touched her nose to the leader's and felt the song surge within her. No longer was it one voice, but many. The image of True-of-voice became overlapped by others—an even grayer male, a pure-white female, and more, who faded into the distance.

See those who came before, said the song. Those who were once True-of-voice—the grandsire, the granddam, the ones in whom the song flowed. They still sing in the one who is now True-of-voice, carrying their wisdom beyond death.

She listened to the song and learned the nature of Quiet Hunter's people.

True-of-voice did not rule the hunters. He did not need to. There was no requirement for obedience. Every act was obedience, because nothing else was possible. The song guided, shaped, and healed. There was nothing else but the song. It filled, it soothed, it brought peace, it brought rapture. One didn't have to want; one didn't even have to have a self to want, for everything needed was given in abundance.

She offered herself gladly in return and rejoiced.

CHAPTER 17

THISTLE HAD EVENTUALLY fallen asleep by Quiet Hunter, and the others had wandered off to nap or groom. But Quiet Hunter lay awake, full of questions that would not go away, even when the song was well heard.

What was behind Thistle's eyes? Sometimes it seemed the same as what lay behind the eyes of his own people. Sometimes it seemed so different.

What makes her give healing and comfort? Quiet Hunter wondered. True-of-voice and the song had no answers for this.

He wanted to give Thistle something in return. So much that it hurt like a bone chip in the belly.

Behind Thistle's eyes lay something that cared for Quiet Hunter. Something more than her voice, the color of her fur, the way she moved, the depth of her gaze.

If she were killed and torn apart to find this thing, he thought, it would not be found.

Sweat came to his paw pads, and prickles woke beneath his fur at the thought that what was behind Thistle's eyes might cease to be if she were killed.

These thoughts were all new, all disturbing. There were no words in the song for them. There never had been.

Thistle stirred and woke up. "Quiet Hunter?" she asked after a while. "Feel I have done something . . . bad to you."

A surge of impatience kept Quiet Hunter silent.

I, I . . . What is this *I*? *I*'s and *if*s and *me*'s. Meaningless!

It was all tangled up. Words, thoughts, everything. No sense was left. The only sense lay in the song.

Go back to it, Quiet Hunter scolded himself. Forget everything else.

"You . . . looking at me in . . . funny way. Why?" Thistle asked, but Quiet Hunter couldn't answer.

Me. Looking . . . at . . . me, he thought. You looking at me. *You* is Quiet Hunter. Looking at is done with the eyes. *Me*—the mystery at the center.

And then, with a quiet shattering, the mystery fell away. It was Thistle. But not just Thistle. *Me* was what was looking out through her eyes. That was what Quiet Hunter wanted in her.

First, he sensed, he had to find it in himself.

He said the word softly. It was dry in his mouth. "Me."

Thistle wanted to stop. This was not the right way for Quiet Hunter. The way of the song was the right way.

But once a hunt like this is begun, it cannot be abandoned, thought Quiet Hunter. He was looking out through his own eyes and speaking new words.

She said, "Your eyes are changing, Quiet Hunter." Thistle sounded regretful, almost fearful. He knew what she was thinking.

I don't want your eyes to change. Go back to where you were meant to be. With True-of-voice. With the song.

But even if you did not want Quiet Hunter's eyes to change, Thistle, you caused it anyway. Just by being what you are, saying the words you say.

Quiet Hunter knew that his eyes had been opened. Even he could not close them again.

CHAPTER 18

IN THE NAMED camp, Ratha watched Bira kindle a morning fire. We don't really need it, Ratha thought, but Bira likes to keep to her routine. Besides, it was good to renew the Red Tongue's embers each day so that they stayed hot.

She turned her thoughts to the face-tails. If the Named wanted one, they would have to capture it before the herd departed, as Thistle said it would. The hunters still would not allow the Named to approach the beasts. Thistle had tried her best, Ratha had to admit, but the differences in understanding between those who followed True-of-voice and those who followed her were too great even for Thistle to cross.

What was the next step? Should the Named take what they needed by means of fire?

Ratha stared at the flames, remembering how she had found the Red Tongue and used it against threats to her people. The choice to use fire had never been easy. This time it was much more difficult.

She wanted to delay, yet she couldn't. All too soon, Thistle had told her, the face-tail herd would start its migration. The hunters would go with it.

If Thistle chose to stay with them, she might go as well. Ratha could not bear to think about that.

As she sat watching the fire, Khushi trotted up with a grouse in his jaws. She stared at him and lifted her tail in a wordless question. When had Khushi learned to hunt?

"Thakur caught it," the scout confessed. "But he's teaching me how. He thought you might like a meal, clan leader."

The growling in Ratha's stomach came more from uneasiness and worry about her daughter than from hunger, but to show her appreciation, she took the grouse and shared it with Bira.

While she was eating, Khushi relayed a report from Thakur. "He thinks that True-of-voice's people will hunt once more before the herd starts to migrate," the scout said. "In fact, he thinks the hunt will happen today."

Ratha sneezed out a mouthful of feathers before she could reply. She left the rest of the grouse to Bira, who was better at dealing with feathered prey.

"We'll join Thakur," she said. "This is a good opportunity."

"To do what, clan leader? We can't catch a face-tail."

"No. I promised Thistle that we wouldn't and I will keep that promise. But the other clan hasn't forbidden us to watch."

Khushi groaned. "That's all I have been doing."

"Well, I want to see how True-of-voice's people hunt. Thakur says they might have picked up some ideas from Thistle."

"Unless they are hunting seamares, I don't know what good her ideas would do them," grumbled Khushi.

Bira raised her muzzle from her feathery meal and spoke quietly. "Thistle knows about more than seamares. She survived by herself for a long time."

"All right, so I'm wrong again," said Khushi. "If we are going to watch, clan leader, let's hurry."

"Sorry to rain on your fur, scout," Ratha said, "but you and Bira are staying here. I only want two of us watching the hunters. They are already wary of us, and I don't want to endanger Thistle. If they get irritated with us, they could turn on her. I may not agree with everything Thistle does, but I realize that she has risked a lot to be accepted by the hunters. Any mistake on our part could ruin everything she's done."

"Then I'll help Bira with the fire," said Khushi, who was never in a bad mood for long.

"If you need help, send for us," said Bira quietly.

Ratha noticed that the Firekeeper and her treeling had laid out resin-filled branches so that firebrands would be quickly available if needed. Bira was probably the most reliable one among the Named, Ratha thought. She rarely made a fuss and she had developed an effective partnership with her treeling, Biaree. They worked so efficiently together that they seemed to be done with tasks before they even started.

I hope I won't need you, Bira, but thank you anyway, Ratha thought as she left.

She met Thakur on the knoll near their camp. At a ground-eating pace he led her up one of the little valleys that opened onto the plain, down a rugged gully, then up and over the top of a ridge of wooded hills. From a viewpoint just below the crest, where the trees thinned out, Ratha saw some face-tails bunched together in a tight group. Behind the great beasts, in a bow-shaped line, were the hunters.

"I've never seen True-of-voice's people do that before," Ratha said, puzzled.

"I haven't either."

They both moved closer, paralleling the hunters and the driven band of prey. Soon Ratha could see that the land was a tilted plateau. The beasts were being driven up-slope.

"There are cliffs ahead," said Thakur. "If the hunters do what I think they are planning, they will drive the herd over the edge."

"The whole herd? That sounds wasteful." The idea of seeing so many of the great beasts crashing down from the drop-off disturbed Ratha. "Are you sure they picked this up from Thistle?"

"The hunters saw what happened when she was being chased by a face-tail. I did, too. She jumped off a bluff and the face-tail followed. The fall wasn't far. Thistle wasn't hurt, but the face-tail was so big and heavy that the fall crippled it. Then it was easy for them to make the kill."

Ratha cantered alongside Thakur, increasing her speed to compensate for his long legs and greater stride. "Thistle said that they didn't learn from outsiders. The only thing they follow is this 'song,' and only True-of-voice can make it."

"Although the song itself comes from True-of-voice, it can include things from any of the others," Thakur said. "Thistle has become part of their group. True-of-voice may walk around in a trance most of his life, but he is not stupid. If he senses something of value in one of his people, he will use it."

"Or misuse it," Ratha added. "I don't like the idea of killing more than you can eat. I wish we'd thought about that before we let Thistle in among them."

Even if we had, would it have made any difference? she wondered. Once I made the decision not to let these hunters alone, I had to find some way of dealing with them. The Red Tongue was one possible way, and Thistle was another. The trouble is, these ways have effects that I can't control.

Ratha and Thakur angled in toward the driven face-tails, staying downwind in the high grass to keep themselves hidden from the hunters. The musty, rank odor of the face-tails was sharp in Ratha's nose. The beasts could not gallop, but their lumbering trot made a rumble that filled the air and shook the ground beneath her paw pads.

The noise grew and swelled, rising like the cloud of rolling dust sent up by the herd. Shrill, brassy trumpeting broke through the thudding rumble, giving voice to the beasts' terror. They were being hunted in a way they had never been hunted before and they knew it.

"Faster," Thakur yowled beside her. "The hunters have got the herd in a stampede." He seemed to sail over the grass as if he were a swift, low-flying bird.

The bawling, the stamping, the thunderous commotion seemed to surround Ratha. For an instant she panicked, thinking that she and Thakur had somehow blundered into the midst of the rampaging animals.

And then Thakur yowled at her again, and she bounded to one side and saw that they were out of the herd's path.

"Ahead . . . the cliff," he panted. "Back there . . . the hunters."

Ratha reared up on her hind legs for a quick look. The bow of hunters around the mass of face-tails was deepening, closing, forcing the animals toward the drop-off. True-of-voice's people might not think and learn in the same way as the Named, but in some ways they were even more effective. Ratha had no doubt that they would kill every face-tail in the group. The thought chilled her spine as she dropped down again beside Thakur.

And it was my Thistle who showed them how.

The dusty haze turned the hunters into a grim line of shadows. She did not want to think that one of them might be her own daughter.

No, Thistle would not be a part of such wasteful killing . . . unless she has been so completely overwhelmed by True-of-voice that she has forgotten herself.

She heard the angry trumpeting of a face-tail turn into an anguished scream. With a rattle of rocks the first animal to reach the cliff plunged over. Another followed, unable to stop. And another and another in a cataract of shaggy fur and flesh, tumbling down with terrible cries and the sounds of heavy flesh meeting stone.

Though the first animals ran over blindly, the ones behind realized their danger and fought to stop. But others collided with them, pushing them over the cliff.

Only the face-tails at the rear of the herd had any chance to veer away or halt their maddened rush.

But the hunters would not allow any to escape. With cold ferocity, they lunged and slashed at the face-tails' legs. Blood mixed with the roiling dust. Some animals tried to use their tusks, but they were too tightly crowded against the bodies of their fellows to do more than toss their heads and flail their trunks.

"Ratha, watch the edge!" Thakur cried. She bounded away with sweaty paw pads, realizing how close she had come to the brink. She crouched with him behind a pile of boulders to one side of the drop-off. Pressed close against him, she felt his sides rise and fall while the smell of carnage drifted up from below the cliff.

Now only three face-tails fought for their lives against the closing ring of hunters: an old bull, a female, and her calf. Relentlessly the hunters pressed them closer to the edge.

Ratha felt herself shiver. True-of-voice's people were already frighteningly effective under his guidance. With the new knowledge gained from Thistle, they were now deadly. She felt a crazy impulse to run between the hunters and their doomed prey. The contest had become too unbalanced, too cruel. . . .

The face-tail bull, his hide gashed by many claws and teeth, backed too close to the cliff edge. The rock and soil crumbled beneath his weight. With a brassy scream he, too, was gone, leaving only the female and her calf to face the hunters.

Her jaws opening in dismay, Ratha stared at True-of-voice, who was at the center of the hunters' line.

Do you have to kill all of them?

But what had been set in motion could not be stopped, even by the one who had created it. The song possessed them all and it was filled with the need to attack and slaughter, even after there was enough meat to fill their bellies many times over.

Thistle had said it. The hunters repeated what they had already done, unable to stop or change. Perhaps that had served them well in the past, but if they continued to hunt like this, they would destroy the prey that sustained them.

But the song would not allow any questions, any doubts.

The face-tail calf screeched in terror as the hunters flanking True-of-voice engulfed it and dragged it away from the enraged mother. The female's roar of anger turned to a roar of grief as the calf's shrilling was abruptly cut off. The shaggy animal charged the hunters twice and was repelled easily, for they were prepared for her desperate attempt to rescue her calf.

What they were not prepared for was the face-tail's attack on True-of-voice. As if the great beast sensed that he was the source of the will that drove the hunters, she turned on him.

Ratha, hidden, saw instantly that True-of-voice had been left dangerously unprotected by the others in their eagerness to bring down the face-tail calf. Now, with yowls of dismay, they sprang to his defense, but too late. The face-tail shook off their attacks. True-of-voice sought to escape, but the flailing, beating trunk found him and wound about his leg.

It flipped the gray leader on his back and dragged him

to the edge of the abyss. Raking the face-tail's forehead with his back claws and twisting around to drive his foreclaws into the rocks and dirt, True-of-voice mounted a frenzied battle.

From behind the hunters' line, Ratha saw two figures charge through—the male called Quiet Hunter and her own Thistle. With a roar, she leaped from cover to her daughter's side. She heard Thakur follow. Flattening her ears, she snaked her head around, ready to launch an attack on anyone who threatened Thistle. No one did. All gazes were locked on the cliff edge, the female face-tail, and True-of-voice.

Slowly, relentlessly, the leader of the hunters was being dragged backward, his claws leaving trails in the dirt. Quiet Hunter and others grabbed him by the scruff and the paws, but the vengeful face-tail was stronger. Her eyes reddened by rage, her black, shaggy pelt stained with blood, the beast wrenched True-of-voice from his rescuers. With a jerk she pulled him to the brink and flung him over.

The face-tail unleashed the rest of her wrath against the ones who had tried to save their leader. Ratha heard Thistle screech in dismay as a vicious downswing of the face-tail's trunk clubbed Quiet Hunter in the ribs and sent him tumbling to one side.

And then, as if she had made her choice, the red-eyed, shaggy-pelted animal pivoted on the brink and let herself topple to join her slaughtered companions below. With a hail of rocks, she was gone, and the dust was already settling on the bloodied and torn ground where True-of-voice had fought for his life.

* * *

To Thistle, the song screamed in a blending of voices high and low. It was True-of-voice himself and all those that sang through him. The fierce hunting sound of the song turned into the sound of terror, a fang thrust through the mind. Then all was bleak and quiet.

She had been in the center of the song, rushing with Quiet Hunter to defend the beloved singer. Now she was snatched away, thrust back into the caverns inside herself. They were no longer jeweled and shimmering with the light of the song. As if a vaulted arch had fallen in, blocking the sun rays from above, all went dark. The shadows took possession. And shadows were where the Dreambiter prowled.

What had been a haven for her was now a threat. She fled outward, as if the rumble behind her were the sound of a cave-in. Yet the paths to the outside, once well-known, had become little-used and forgotten. Like the hunters, she, too, was trapped, and though she ran to the side of the beloved one who had fallen under the face-tail's strike, she could not break through to him. She could only fling herself against the inward walls that would not yield to either panic or rage. And soon, close behind her, she heard the echoing growl of the Dreambiter.

The battle was over. Finished. Ratha let out the breath she was holding, moved legs that felt as though they had been frozen. Thakur was already urging her away silently, with pressure from his body. She resisted, looking frantically for Thistle. Her daughter was there, crouching beside a breathless and dazed Quiet Hunter.

The other hunters looked dazed, too, even though they hadn't been struck by the face-tail. They milled in confusion at the edge of the drop-off, as if unable to comprehend what had happened.

In an instant everything had changed. True-of-voice was gone. Had the song gone with him?

Ratha saw the answer in the shocked and stricken look in Thistle's eyes, in the way Quiet Hunter, who had been the bravest of the hunters in his attempt to free True-of-voice, now lay shaking and helpless on the ground.

True-of-voice was gone. Without him as the source of the song that moved and shaped their actions, the hunters were as helpless as newborn cubs.

Ratha felt a bleakness within her and a sense of horror as she watched the hunters turn to one another, lost and frightened, perhaps for the first time in their lives. And Thistle . . . her Thistle . . . shared their loss, their agony. Thistle's agony was overwhelming her as well. Ratha knew how deeply her daughter cared for Quiet Hunter.

But isn't this what you wanted; isn't this what you worked for? a voice spoke inside her. You said you wanted the hunters dead. Without True-of-voice, they essentially are. There is no opposition now. The Named will prevail.

She suddenly wished that things had not happened this way. True-of-voice did not deserve this. Nor did his people. Nor her daughter.

Thakur moved closer to her, silently communicating his presence, his support. He was the one who knew Thistle best. She wanted to ask him to go to her daughter and offer the comfort that she could not.

Let him comfort her so that I can back away . . . again, she thought miserably. But then suddenly something flamed up inside her, as hot and strong as the Red Tongue itself. No. I'm not going to shy away from her any longer. I care too much about her.

Ratha glanced warily at the hunters, wondering if she should avoid them, but they were all so preoccupied with the loss of their leader that they could only sit and stare or walk in dazed circles. All she got was a puzzled look or a halfhearted growl as she made her way through them toward her daughter.

Thistle, who had been crouching beside Quiet Hunter, raised her muzzle and stared directly at Ratha. It was hard for Ratha to keep walking toward her, to keep gazing into her eyes. Her overwhelming urge was to veer off, to drop her gaze, to run.

But Ratha met the sea-green stare and felt the grief deep within it. Forgetting everything else, she bounded to her daughter. With a wild flurry of her heart, she saw Thistle leap toward her—not to attack in protest or anger, but to bury her head against Ratha's chest.

Flinging her paws about her daughter, the leader of the Named gathered Thistle to her, holding her fiercely.

Thistle, my cub, my walker on strange trails. Come to me. Whatever harms you, I will fight it; whatever hurts you, I will heal it. I am the one who birthed you and wounded you. Now let me help you.

The thickness in her throat made her half purr, half growl as she said softly, "Tell me."

Thistle's voice was ragged, broken. Her ribs heaved as she gasped, "True-of-voice. The song. Ended. Everything. Gone. Lost. Left only . . . hurt."

"Not everything has ended for you," Ratha said. "I know you care about Quiet Hunter and his people. I know the song was important, even if I didn't understand it."

"Can't live if song ends!" Thistle cried, barely able to speak. Her eyes were swirling, her pupils remote. She began to shake, with the same sort of shuddering that was racking Quiet Hunter. Thakur was crouched down beside the young male, trying all his healing skills to soothe and calm him.

"Yes you can," Ratha said, gently but firmly. "You can walk both their trails and ours. Come back from the strange trails, my Named one."

"Not Named," Thistle said in a low moan. "Inside, no names, no knowing." Her voice faltered, faded.

Ratha sensed that her daughter was slipping into the same abyss of helpless despair that was claiming the hunters. With a rising despair of her own, she knew she would lose Thistle. Unless . . .

"Thistle-chaser. That is your name. I gave it to you. I'll be meat for maggots if I let you refuse it! As Named and leader of the Named, I command you to come back to me, my Thistle-chaser."

But the only answer was in the strangely swirling eyes with their shifting green sea.

In the endless dark, where dread sent her fleeing toward madness, something suddenly loomed ahead. Not so much seen, but heard and felt. Her name, spoken in her mother's voice.

Her name shone ahead. Thistle. Thistle-chaser. Named and spoken and known.

She who could run on many paths remembered the ones she had run among the Named. She launched herself toward the inside cavern wall that had once been unyielding and suddenly she was through, from inside herself to outside, from ocean into air, from entrancement to awareness. She gasped, taking a huge breath as if she had risen from beneath a murky sea into sharp, clear air.

She blinked as if she had indeed been swimming in the salt ocean instead of a sea of the mind. But what stung her like ocean brine and made her eyes run was not salt, but mixed joy and grief.

Joy because she felt her mother's caring, the power in the forelegs that embraced her, the fire of body and spirit that surrounded her, the raw devotion in a voice that said she was Named and known and deeply loved. . . .

Grief as well, because outside the protective circle that Ratha and Thakur formed about her, she saw True-of-voice's people. Some were pacing in circles, others huddled and shuddering like Quiet Hunter. Some were in mindless fights, as if what they had just lost had been stolen and could be wrestled back.

She could run on paths inside and outside. The dream-walking hunters could not. They were trapped inside, in caverns that had once echoed with the beauty of the song, but now held only emptiness.

They who were fearless killers were now parentless

cubs. For them the world had become a wilderness, the wind keening with unanswered questions.

And among them, trapped in emptiness, was Quiet Hunter.

When she pushed gently against her mother's clasp, Ratha let her go and, apparently understanding, gave her a gentle nudge toward Quiet Hunter. Thakur gave her a brief welcoming lick, then moved aside to let her get close to the stricken young male.

Thistle tried to reach out to Quiet Hunter in the way she had done before, in the way she knew that True-of-voice had once done. She sensed a wounded bleakness in him, as if something had reached cruelly inside and torn out the core of his being.

She crouched beside Quiet Hunter, rubbing against him, licking him, trying to warm him with her body, move him with her voice. Trying to bring him outside to where there was life, even if it was bare and no longer enfolded by the rapture of the song. To where there was light, even if it was clear, sharp, and cold.

But there was no path for Quiet Hunter to the outside, she sensed sadly. The only trail was one she herself had showed him. He had ventured along it only a short way before turning back.

She knew, in the bareness and clearness and coldness of life, that the end of the song meant the end of being for Quiet Hunter and his kind. Not for her. With her mother's gift of name and knowing, she could jump the abyss of loss and despair, or bridge it with her two states of being. Quiet Hunter had only one. His approach to the chasm would be a plunge into death.

CHAPTER 19

✳ IN THE SETTLING dust, Thakur stood over Quiet Hunter, nosing him gently. With a grunt of surprise, he said, "I thought he was dead, Ratha, but he's not. Maybe I can help him."

Ratha, with one paw around her daughter, said, "Thistle came back. Maybe he can, too."

"No," Thistle cried, her voice muffled because her nose was once more buried against Ratha's chest. "Maybe I can come back, but Quiet Hunter can't. He knows no trails other than the ways of the song. For him . . . everything is ended."

And you cry out in agony because you want to help him just as I want to help you, Ratha thought.

Ratha was not sure whether she felt stunned, shocked, saddened, or relieved by what had happened. She was, for the moment, thankful that the hunters were too stricken and confused to cause trouble for the Named, although she knew that might end soon. Right now it was Thistle who needed her badly.

Her daughter's eyes were filled with agony as she gazed at Quiet Hunter. "Their pain . . . his pain . . . my fault," Thistle moaned. "Showed his people . . .

bad way to kill face-tails. Didn't mean to. But couldn't hide from True-of-voice. Became part of the song, but learning not complete enough."

The words were jumbled, but Ratha understood them. Firmly she answered, though her voice was threatening to shake as much as Thistle's, "It wasn't your fault. I won't let you blame yourself."

"Happened . . . because I became one of them."

"It happened because of what you are and what they are. I was the one who said you could try. And it worked, Thistle. You became one who could walk on both trails, theirs and ours. So we could speak instead of fighting."

"Cared much . . . for Quiet Hunter. Didn't want to hurt him."

"I know," Ratha said softly. "Thakur is trying to heal him."

Thistle's voice broke in a sob as she watched Thakur crouching over Quiet Hunter. "Kindness . . . caring . . . from the Named, even Thakur . . . not enough. Only the song can heal Quiet Hunter. Song died with True-of-voice."

Again Ratha drew Thistle to her.

Suddenly Thistle gave a strange gasp, and her pupils widened. She pulled away from Ratha. "No . . . Can't be. Thought it came again . . . an instant. No. Imagining because I want it. Not real. Only hope."

"What is it?"

"The song. Thought I . . . heard. . . . No. Can't be. Can't be. Not if True-of-voice is dead."

Looking at the intense expression on her daughter's face, Ratha wondered if Thistle's longing was responsible for what she now sensed. That would be one way to face the situation. Yet she had learned enough about her daughter to know that Thistle would not delude herself.

Thistle gave an odd little twitch, as if something had touched her. She looked to her mother, a question forming in the depths of her eyes.

Ratha looked back, her gaze steady. "You are all assuming that True-of-voice is dead. Maybe he isn't."

A tangle of conflicting thoughts made Ratha's belly churn as she followed Thistle to the edge of the cliff where True-of-voice had fallen. Things were happening too fast. She felt as though she were being jerked one way and then another.

It had been easy to find sympathy for Quiet Hunter's people when she thought that the source of their power and direction was gone. In the instant that they had become vulnerable, they were no longer alien, no longer enemy. The Named, too, had experienced loss. At least they had that much in common.

Now, with the chance that True-of-voice still lived, Ratha felt that she was on much more treacherous ground. She could no longer return to her previous stance of viewing Quiet Hunter's people as completely alien and easy to hate. Now things were more complex. Thistle and Quiet Hunter had shown that there was shared ground with her own people. Ratha could not and would not deny that.

Yet if True-of-voice lived, the leader of the Named would have to be on her guard. She had to keep the interests of her own clan foremost. The hunters had already shown that they could be frighteningly power-ful. And if there was a chance that they could regain True-of-voice . . .

This is not going to be easy. I want to help Thistle and Quiet Hunter without betraying the Named.

She looked ahead to where Thistle crouched, peering down over the cliff edge. Near Thistle the ground and the scrub bushes were trampled or torn up. There were dark blood spatters drying in the dust.

"Here. This is where he fell," Thistle said, her voice flat.

Ratha felt a shiver as she passed between blank-eyed hunters who could only stare at her dully. She felt a surge of scorn mixed with revulsion. They had all given up. Just like that. Take away their powerful leader, and their initiative died.

In that way, they were very different from the Named. If my people lost me, they would grieve, but they would choose someone else and go on.

And even before the other clan had confirmed that their leader was really dead, they had fallen apart. Thistle was right. These people seemed to get stuck or paralyzed in the strangest ways. Didn't anyone even look to see if True-of-voice might have landed on a ledge or some-thing below?

She found herself curling one side of her lip up over her fangs. How could she respect these people? They really could not think for themselves. They had to be told what to do. Even trivial things. Everything was ruled by True-of-voice, through the strange, uni-fying bond of something Thistle could only call "the song."

I hate it. I hate even the idea of it.

Ratha crouched beside Thistle and peered over, studying the rock face that dropped away from the edge beneath her feet. It looked pretty sheer . . . yet there were some ledges. And some bushes growing right out of the rocks, which someone might catch and cling to in desperation. And halfway down there was a shelf and something dark on the shelf. . . .

Ratha's heart began to pound. Could it be? Or was her imagination painting that sprawled cat-form on the rocks below?

The shape lay still. It would do the hunters no good to recover True-of-voice if he was dead.

But Thistle had felt . . . something. A brief echo of the song? Was it just self-delusion or was it real? Ratha knew her kind were tough. She herself had survived wounds and falls. Thistle had once run right off a cliff during one of her strange fits and had not even been badly hurt.

There was only one way to find out whether True-of-voice still clung to life.

Ratha herself could not run the paths to where the answer lay.

Her eyes met her daughter's. She did not have to ask Thistle to leave the trails of the Named for those of Quiet Hunter's people. She could see that Thistle was already journeying inward, seeking the source of the song.

And at last, when she came back, her eyes were wide with astonishment. "It is there," she whispered. "Oh, so faint. But it is there. True-of-voice lives."

* * *

Thistle was not the only one who could sense the flickering flame of life on the ledge below, although she was the most sensitive, Ratha noted. Only after she had led Ratha to the cliff edge did some of the hunters start to drift in the same direction. True-of-voice's feeble call had reached them too—Ratha could tell by the startled expressions of hope that broke through the dull resignation.

But his touch was weak and sporadic. Ratha could almost read the resurgence and waning of his strength in the eyes of his people. And in her daughter's eyes as well.

Gradually the hunters at the top of the cliff gathered in a cluster, as if they were moving as close as they could to True-of-voice. Those at the bottom, who had begun halfheartedly eating the carcasses of the slaughtered face-tails, abandoned their kills and crowded to the base of the cliff, staring up at their marooned and dying leader.

To Ratha's surprise, Thakur's skill, or the tenuous return of the song, or both, had revived Quiet Hunter enough so that the young male could stagger to the cliff edge. Ratha had an instant of alarm when she thought he was going to stumble right over, but both Thistle and Thakur blocked Quiet Hunter and pushed him firmly back.

True-of-voice's people gazed down at their leader with forlorn expressions and drooping whiskers. Even those whose age should have given them some wisdom looked as lost as the yearlings. And at the bottom of the rock face, more of the grieving clan looked up in hopeful and hopeless longing.

They know they can't reach him, Ratha thought. They know he is dying. They can feel it.

For Ratha it was a heartbreaking yet eerie scene as more and more of the hunters gathered, as if to hold vigil for their lost leader.

No. He is more than their leader, Ratha thought. He is their life.

To command such devotion . . . Ratha felt a strange flash of envy toward the distant True-of-voice. To be so loved . . . without hesitation or question.

She glanced at her daughter, who was sitting beside the crouching Quiet Hunter. Thistle had laid her paw gently on his back, as if to make sure that he would not lean too far over the cliff in his attempt to get closer to True-of-voice.

Thistle was trembling, her eyes closed. She who could be safe "outside" had chosen to go within, to share the grief and suffering of Quiet Hunter's people. Yet she was not totally entranced, for she pressed down harder on her paw each time a surge of grief made Quiet Hunter try to crawl dangerously close to the drop-off.

Ratha found herself wishing that she had even a tiny part of Thistle's strange gift . . . so that she, too, could share in the powerful emotion that was binding the other clan even closer to their leader. Yet she knew she would always be watching from outside. Even if she had the ability, she would not use it.

The gift of the Named, the one that had so shaped her people, was wakeful awareness. Ratha knew it was

so precious to her that she would fight and kill to preserve it. She already had.

We who are Named will never walk in dreams, she
thought, with a strange mixture of pride and sorrow.
Except for Thistle.

She felt someone coming alongside her. Familiar fur
rubbed against her own and a wonderfully familiar smell
replaced the odors of mourning strangers. Thakur.
Wonderfully Named, sensible, wide-awake Thakur.

She leaned against him with a grateful sigh. For a
while he seemed to be content to provide quiet companionship, but then he spoke in a calm, yet serious voice.
"Clan leader, we probably should take Thistle and back
off a bit. I'm starting to get some resentful looks."

"I don't think she'll come. Not while Quiet Hunter—"
Ratha broke off. Yes, some of the hunters were sending
distinctly black looks in their direction. She knew how easily grief could flare into rage. And it could be argued that
the Named had indirectly caused the tragedy.

"All right," she heard Thakur say. "Thistle should
be safe, but it would be better if we retreated."

Ratha did not want the reminder that as long as True-
of-voice remained alive, the hunters were a threat.

She agreed to back off, but insisted on staying near
enough to keep an eye on her daughter. They took cover
in some brush that had not been trampled.

"How long do you think they will stay?" she asked
Thakur.

"Until True-of-voice dies," he replied softly.

"It may take days!"

"I know. He was strong."

After those words Thakur was quiet for so long that Ratha was startled when he spoke again.

"Clan leader, how do you feel about this?"

She found it very difficult to answer him. On the one side, the Named would benefit if True-of-voice's death destroyed the hunters. No one would stand in the way and the Named could take all the face-tails they wanted. On the other, she understood too well the wrenching impact of the tragedy.

"It helps us," she said at last. "If only Thistle weren't caught up in it."

Thakur looked toward the other clan. "Thistle told me that their leaders are usually older and have cubs that can succeed them. True-of-voice had a mate, but she was killed before she had her first litter."

"This must have happened before," Ratha protested. "They can't be so ridiculously vulnerable or they wouldn't have survived."

"Maybe things are changing for them, clan leader."

Perhaps things are. And perhaps we are part of the change. The idea was not comforting.

She had a sudden odd thought. Would I help them if I could?

She stared out at True-of-voice's people. They were drawn so strongly by the need for their leader that they risked falling from the cliff. And her daughter was sitting among them, one paw still on the male called Quiet Hunter.

I don't know.

The vigil for True-of-voice continued. Weariness at last made Ratha and Thakur withdraw to their own camp, but the following day, she moved the base so that she could be closer to Thistle. She and Bira were careful to site it downwind of the mourning clan so that the smoke of the Red Tongue would not alarm them.

Although they are so wrapped up in True-of-voice that they wouldn't notice, she thought as she helped Bira gather tinder for the fire.

The next question Ratha thought of was one she had trouble answering. How long would the group remain there? Certainly until True-of-voice died; but what would happen once they were leaderless?

She suspected that they would continue with the vigil, even after it had become pointless. Without direction, they might stay there indefinitely. And Thistle—how long would Thistle stay with them?

Probably as long as Quiet Hunter survives, she thought, feeling her throat tighten. She had learned how painful it was to lose someone beloved. Ratha's chosen mate, and Thistle's father, Bonechewer, had died in the struggle between the Named and their enemies. Now her daughter would soon know the same loss.

She tried to shake herself free of the impending tragedy. She had to look ahead, into the future. The Named had come to capture face-tails. The hunters had blocked them. Now, with the other clan paralyzed and distracted, there would be no more interference.

At an evening gathering around the Named campfire, everyone talked about what to do next. Khushi felt that the Named should make another try to capture a face-tail. The five of them had already been here far longer than intended. Fessran and the others would be starting to worry. Bira agreed. She was also getting restless.

Thakur, however, urged caution. The hunters, he said, might not be as paralyzed as they seemed. Grief and frustration could easily ignite into rage. If the bereaved group did not lash out against the Named directly, they might well take out their anger on the Named one who remained among them—Thistle.

Ratha, torn, agreed on a compromise. On the following day the Named would prepare for another attempt to capture a face-tail, but the hunt itself would not take place until the day after.

She needed to find a way to either get Thistle back from the hunters or minimize the threat to her daughter. Given Thistle's determination, she wouldn't return until True-of-voice died. Or Quiet Hunter.

If she even comes back at all. She may hate me for letting this happen to the hunters and then not doing anything to help. But I have no choice. Or do I?

Before Ratha could make any definite plans or carry them out, however, the hunters showed that they might be grief-stricken, but not rendered completely helpless.

The morning after the campfire meeting, Ratha woke to find Khushi and Thakur gone. Sounds of yowling and spitting from the bottom of the cliff told her that the situation had erupted into a fight.

Telling Bira to take a torch and follow, she galloped toward the foot of the cliff, where the second group of hunters was gathered, waiting for the death of their leader. Remembering Thakur's warning, she feared the worst.

Before she and Bira were even halfway there, a brown streak shot past her and down the trail. It was Khushi, running as if all the hunters were after him. An instant later, there was the flash of a copper coat, and Thakur dashed into view.

Bira, her torch burning fiercely in her jaws, leaped forward to attack any enemy that might be pursuing him.

"No!" Ratha heard Thakur yowl. "Run. Don't fight. They won't go far from True-of-voice."

Although Ratha felt ready for a good scrap, she turned around, and Bira followed.

As the three fled together down the trail, Ratha cantered abreast of Thakur, asking what had happened.

"It was that idiot Khushi," Thakur panted. "He tried to take some meat from a face-tail carcass."

They caught up with Khushi near the camp. The scout was abashed, yet defiant.

"I was hungry," he confessed. "And I was tired of eating grouse. The face-tail meat was just lying there, attracting vultures. I didn't think they would care. They weren't eating it."

"So you sneaked in there and got the hunters all stirred up," Ratha snarled. "I should shred your ears and maybe a few more parts!"

Khushi looked sheepish. "I—I didn't think they cared. They didn't seem to notice me. At least at first. Then, yarr! They were all over me!"

"And you would have been another piece of meat for the vultures if Thakur hadn't gone in after you."

"I guess I would have," the young scout said shakily. Turning almost shyly to Thakur, he said, "I'm grateful, herding teacher. I don't know why I thought I could get away with it. Perhaps it was because they didn't seem to notice me, even when I was right at the kill. Then all of a sudden . . ." He trailed off.

"They don't give warning signals," said Thakur shortly, licking a deep scratch on his foreleg. "That is why what you did was so dangerous."

Ratha interrupted. "We can't stay here talking. I want to make sure your stupid blunder didn't make the hunters turn on Thistle."

Khushi's eyes opened wide. "Oh no! I didn't realize . . . Well, she's in the other group at the top of the cliff, isn't she?"

"Scout, next time try thinking with your brain, not your guts. Guts are for stuffing with food and making dung. Not for thinking with," Ratha said brusquely. "Remember that the next time."

Khushi gulped. "I—I'm sorry, clan leader. I hope Thistle is safe."

"So do I," Ratha said curtly.

With Khushi, Bira, and Thakur close behind, she headed for the trail to the cliff top.

Sitting among True-of-voice's people, her paw still on Quiet Hunter, Thistle felt her exhaustion and desperation grow as True-of-voice's song faded.

It had changed several times during the night. First it had spoken of suffering, then of fear for the fate of those it was abandoning. Early in the morning there had also been a strong flash of rage at the doings of the strangers, and Thistle feared that her mother had led the Named across some forbidden boundary.

Now the song had changed for the final time. Now it was saying farewell.

It had grown so weak that many could not hear it. Quiet Hunter was among them. He still lay, like many others, with his nose at the cliff edge. He was no longer trying to crawl over. The call that drew him had faded from his mind. Thistle kept her paw on his back, to keep him beside her and to tell him wordlessly that she still heard the waning thread of the song.

As long as he understood, he would fight to stay alive. As long as he knew that the song continued, even in someone else's mind, he would not bury himself in the lost blackness of his own.

Thistle wondered how much longer he would struggle if she kept her paw on him after the song had faded out completely. Would it be worth having him beside her for a little more time if she had to lie to him?

No, she thought, and the paw on Quiet Hunter's back trembled, for the song was getting harder to hear.

She caught glances from some of the others around her. She knew they were watching her, waiting for the moment she would take her paw from Quiet Hunter's back. The looks were starting to get resentful, and unspoken questions seemed to gather in the air around her.

Why can she still hear True-of-voice when we cannot? We are his people—why do we have to listen to an outsider?

Don't know where I got this gift. Never wanted it, she answered back silently. She did not speak aloud lest it distract her. Even thinking the words loosened her grip on the last fading vestiges of the song, and she had to scramble wildly to keep hold of it.

And now the mutters were starting.

"The song is not heard. True-of-voice is dead."

"That one says he is not dead. The paw is on Quiet Hunter."

"The paw does not work. The tongue does not work. They say things are so when they are not. That is a bad thing."

"That one made the first face-tail fall off a cliff. The face-tail died. True-of-voice saw. Then the song commanded that other face-tails be killed that way."

"The song changed because of what that one did. It caused hurt. True-of-voice is lost."

"That one" felt her fur start to prickle in apprehension. Her ears twitched back. She wished she could speak her feelings as clearly as she thought them. Was all a mistake. Never meant to show True-of-voice anything. Was all an accident. When I jumped off the bluff, the face-tail followed.

"The song would not cause hurt. Those who hear would not cause hurt. Outsiders do. That one has caused hurt. That one is an outsider, a stranger."

Thistle felt her eyes starting to flame with rage. Whose fault was it that the tragedy happened? Who chose to copy her, even though the face-tail's death was an accident? True-of-voice himself. He made all the decisions for the group. He laid his will on his people. He had created his own downfall.

She struggled to put away the anger and the urge to protest aloud. It would do no good. And distractions would only hasten the moment when she lost the last tenuous filament of the song and had to lift her paw from Quiet Hunter's back.

"Those who stay with harmful ones also cause hurt. Quiet Hunter stays with the stranger."

This time Thistle could not help turning her head to give the speaker a hard stare. She could accept the slights against herself, but not against Quiet Hunter. He had done nothing wrong. And he was, perhaps, enduring more than any of them, for he refused to take refuge in rage and hatred.

Oh, gentle one, beloved one. Wish you would get angry. Even anger against me, I could bear. Would know then that you choose to struggle rather than suffer.

She heard more mutters. Those who were sitting near her drew away.

"She killed True-of-voice. Drive her out."

"Drive Quiet Hunter out, too. He is with her."

Tension and fear snapped Thistle's concentration. She felt the song slip away. It was no good to pretend.

Quickly she bent to whisper in Quiet Hunter's ear. "Can't hear song anymore. Leader isn't dead. Just can't reach him. Everyone so angry, noisy. Understand?"

Dully he replied, "It is understood."

She took her paw from his back just as one of the others took an aggressive step toward her. The low background mutter grew into a rumble, then a roar.

"Drive her out! Drive him out!"

Drive us out from what? she thought, wishing she could speak to them as eloquently as she did to herself. You have nothing left. All you had was True-of-voice, and he will soon be gone.

She suddenly felt a deep pity for the hunters. Forlorn, lost, they were reaching for anything that might comfort them. Even hate.

Calmly she said, "Leader still lives. But you so noisy, angry. Makes him hard to hear."

"Hear her speak!" someone yowled. "The song does not know those words. Stranger! Stranger! Slayer of the song!"

Thistle had seen how the creature the Named called the Red Tongue could spread swiftly through dry wood. With equal speed rage flared up in the group as they yowled and chanted the same words over and over. "Stranger, stranger, slayer of the song. Bleed for True-of-voice. Die for True-of-voice."

Feeling her fur rising all over, Thistle backed away from those closing in on her. "Will go," she snarled. "But leave Quiet Hunter alone."

"No. He has been made a stranger."

"He is mated to the slayer of the song." The voices were ugly. Teeth were starting to show.

Before Thistle could say anything else, claws flashed in a stroke across Quiet Hunter's side. Her own rage leaped up and it was all she could do to keep from flinging herself at the attacker.

If I fight, I'll die. If I leave him, he'll die. With her jaws, she grabbed Quiet Hunter's scruff. Startled by the sudden pain of the claw slash, he was fighting his way out of his trance. Someone else raked his flank. He screamed and shuddered, but whirled to face them, jerking away from Thistle's hold.

"No, run!" she hissed at him. "With me. Away."

The look of horror that he gave her told her that the idea of leaving his people was so shattering that he was paralyzed.

"Hunters will kill you," she cried, and rammed her body into him, forcing him to stagger a few steps away.

Her heart cried out for him. He had done nothing wrong except allow her to care for him.

The look in Quiet Hunter's eyes told Thistle that he knew he had no choice and, unfairly or not, he was being cast out. On top of the pain of losing the song, he was losing everything else he knew.

Fending off flurries of slashes and bites, he backed away until he was alongside Thistle. She could barely meet his stricken glance.

"So wrong. Because of me," she whispered.

"Life here is ended," Quiet Hunter said, his voice dead. "Lead, Thistle."

And when she bounded away, he followed.

As Ratha galloped along the upper reaches of the cliff trail, she heard the sound of someone descending. The noises of fighting had already drifted to her from above, making her belly jump with fear for her daughter.

She was about to leave the trail and leap into the bushes when she recognized the pattern of the approaching footsteps.

"Thistle," she said.

Thakur, running beside her, cocked his ears. "Somebody's with her."

"Or chasing her." Ratha felt a growl creep into her voice. She readied herself to defend her daughter if necessary.

Rocks broke loose on the switchback above, and Ratha saw a pair of sea-green eyes glow. Another pair, golden yellow, shone from the face of the form behind her.

"Who is that?" Khushi hissed in surprise.

"I can guess," Ratha heard Thakur answer. "Quiet Hunter."

But Ratha was looking only at the sea-green eyes and smelling the scent of her daughter as Thistle came down the last stretch of trail. Then a familiar set of whiskers brushed hers; a small, sinewy body rubbed briefly alongside; and a voice breathed a single word: "Mother."

Ratha felt a warm tingling sweep over her as she rubbed her head against Thistle's flank, eyes closed in happiness. "My cub. My strong, brave, clever daughter."

"Is anyone following you two?" Thakur asked.

"No," Thistle replied. "Hunters don't go far from True-of-voice."

"So he is still alive?" Ratha said, surprised.

"Think so. Everyone around me noisy, angry. Couldn't hear him anymore. Chased me away. Chased Quiet Hunter too. Wasn't right."

Ratha saw Thistle turn to her companion. The male with the yellow-gold eyes had been silent, but the look in those eyes told Ratha more than any words.

He has been torn out of his world and thrown into ours. I have never seen anyone look so lost.

"Resting place not far," she heard Thistle say to him in a gentle tone of voice her daughter rarely used. "Can keep going?"

"Can. Have to," he answered.

Thistle gave him an encouraging lick. "Know how hard for Quiet Hunter. Care. Very much."

"The pace can be kept slow," Ratha offered, trying to omit any words that would jar Quiet Hunter. "No one is following."

"Weariness is not in the paws. Weariness is in the place behind the eyes." Quiet Hunter's voice was remote.

His last words completely baffled Ratha. She decided that it would be better to let Thistle talk to him, at least for now.

At a slow trot, she set off toward the camp.

CHAPTER 20

LATER THAT EVENING, Thistle, dozing beside Quiet Hunter, raised her chin from her paws. She saw the glow of the Red Tongue through the trees. All of the Named were curled up near the fire, except for Khushi, who had volunteered for sentry duty. She and Quiet Hunter slept at a distance from the campfire. She had told Ratha that Quiet Hunter had already been jolted enough without having to cope with seeing and smelling the Red Tongue close up. The flame might be her mother's creature, but to Thistle it was still a threat.

Even away from the campfire, Quiet Hunter remained too tense to sleep. Every time he started to drop off, something seemed to jerk him awake again.

"This is the first time that Quiet Hunter has tried to fall asleep without hearing the song," he confessed, his voice miserable. "Quiet Hunter forgets, drowses, drifts inside, seeking the warm, comfortable place where the song used to be. But there is only bleakness, coldness. As if Quiet Hunter has fallen into icy water." He paused.

Thistle felt herself shivering. She knew in part how he was feeling. The song that had come from True-of-voice had given her so much. To have it suddenly yanked away had been painful even to her. How much more agonizing it must be to someone who had known and depended on it his entire life!

"It will never come again," Quiet Hunter said, and Thistle ached at the heavy resignation in his voice.

"Don't know," she answered, feeling helpless.

"Quiet Hunter cannot live in icy water. Quiet Hunter cannot sleep in icy water."

"Quiet Hunter," Thistle said, and paused to lick him gently. She would do anything for him and she wanted to be with him. She had never felt this way about anybody else, neither her mother nor Thakur.

Yet Quiet Hunter could be beside her now only because he had been torn from his own people and from a way of being that was his life. He knew nothing else.

"Is everything . . . icy water?" she asked, hoping for and dreading the answer.

But the one she cared for only lay and stared ahead without speaking.

Now that Ratha had Thistle back, she felt she could start to capture face-tails for the Named herds. But the Named could not even get near the face-tails. Each time they tried, they were driven back with such ferocity that they could only tuck under their tails and run. Soon everyone bore wounds from the repeated attempts.

Each retreat made Ratha angrier. And each new gash, bite, or scratch on one of her people seemed to hurt her just as much. Khushi and Bira urged her to fight back using the Red Tongue. At first she refused, but seeing the frustration and suffering among those in her band, she began to reconsider.

"All I am doing is prolonging this," she answered impatiently when Thakur asked her to think again before she acted. "The hunters have no right to keep us from taking face-tails. I have no more patience with them. If we can end their interference by using the Red Tongue, then we should."

The herding teacher answered, "I would still move carefully, clan leader. And do not make the mistake of underestimating them. They could take the Red Tongue and use it against us."

Ratha disagreed. "They can barely get themselves organized enough to drive us away. Without True-of-voice, they are falling apart. It's not a pretty thing to watch, but nothing we can do will change what happens to them."

"So if they sit and rot, it is no doing of ours." Thakur's voice had an edge to it. "And you think there is nothing wrong with hastening things a little with the Red Tongue."

"I am doing what is necessary to protect my own people," Ratha snapped. "If the hunters would leave us alone, I wouldn't have to."

"If we had left *them* alone, this wouldn't have happened."

Ratha felt her ears twitch back. "Thakur, I can't deal with *what ifs*. I have to cope with what has actually happened."

"That is what I am trying to say," said Thakur, but Ratha was too irritated to answer him, and at last he sighed and went away.

★ ★ ★

For Quiet Hunter, Thistle and daylight arrived together. The eyes had opened on a new world.

No. The words were not right, he thought. *My* eyes have opened on a new world. Thistle's face and everything that surrounds it.

He blinked.

So this is the world outside the song. It is the same as I have always known, but now bathed in a hard, aching light.

Here, there is only one behind the eyes. One looking out. In the song, there were many—beyond counting. All, alive and dead, sang through True-of-voice.

Now there is only one. That is what makes the light hard and aching.

He knew that Thistle could get close, but however much she rubbed or lay against him, she could not get inside.

His throat caught with a strange new pain.

The pain came from feeling stripped bare of fur and even of skin. So tender that even a soft paw stroke hurt. It was never that way within the song. It enfolded all of us. But the song ended. The choice was either death or this.

He wanted to cry aloud, Thistle, how do you bear it? What is your word for being only one behind the eyes?

Awake? No.

Alone.

Ratha was still brooding over Thakur's words when she saw Thistle approach her. She watched her daughter with mixed feelings. The events of the previous days had drawn them closer together than Ratha had thought possible, but she knew Thistle would oppose any decision to defend the interests of the Named with fire.

With a heavy feeling in her stomach, Ratha wished she were not clan leader. Or that Thistle could separate the Ratha who was her mother from the one who fought to preserve her people at any cost.

"How is Quiet Hunter?" Ratha asked.

"Hurting. Tired. For him to follow our trails . . . he has to fight his own nature."

Ratha knew that she meant much more than the trails that led to the Named camp.

"He is welcome to live among us if he wants," she offered.

"Don't know if he can. Needs True-of-voice. The song. Thought that me caring for him would be enough. May not be, though." Thistle sighed.

I want to ask if there is anything I can do to help Quiet Hunter. But what Thistle would say would oppose the decision I have to make.

"Quiet Hunter is not a weakling," Thistle said abruptly. "Not a coward."

Ratha cocked her head. "Did anyone say he was?"

"No, but can see it in Khushi's eyes. Even in Bira's. Even in yours, a little bit."

"I'm sorry," Ratha said, startled by the accusation. "I have been trying not to judge him. It isn't easy."

"None of you could do what he has done," Thistle said passionately. "Everything is new trails to him. Has to change ways of speaking, ways of thinking. Even way of being, right down to the core. Not something a weakling or coward could do. Would go screaming crazy at the confusion."

Ratha tried to speak calmly, yet she felt herself bracing for a confrontation. "Thistle. You want something from me. Is it the same thing that Thakur wants?"

Her daughter looked back at her.

"No. Thakur wants that you not use Red Tongue against Quiet Hunter's people. I want more. Want you to help them."

Thistle's voice was quiet, yet determined. Ratha felt her own start to rise in frustration.

"Help them? How?"

"Save True-of-voice."

"Thistle, it is too late. He's dead. And even if he wasn't—"

The small yet powerful voice interrupted Ratha's stream of objections. "Not dead. Have felt things like little flutters. Heard things like cries in the distance. They say he is not dead."

"But it has been several days since he fell. How could he possibly be alive?"

She was startled again at Thistle's eloquence as her daughter said, "If you are . . . center and soul of your people; if you are . . . source of everything they need . . . if you know that when you die they will have nothing, then you fight to the last against death." Thistle paused. "You are leader. You would do same for Named ones if they needed you so much."

Again Ratha stared at her daughter, floored by the mixture of bluntness and desperation in Thistle's words.

She is right. I would do it for the Named. I would do it for her, too, but she finds it hard to believe that.

"So you think that . . . concern . . . for his people . . . is keeping True-of-voice alive?"

"Do not think. Know."

"Thistle, even if he is still alive and what you feel is not in your own imagination, what can we do?"

"Save him."

"How?"

"Do not know," Thistle admitted. She lifted her head and stared deep into Ratha's eyes. "Only know that when you Named ones decide to do something, you figure out a way."

Ratha let her hindquarters drop and sat down, feeling overwhelmed by the demand. But was it so unfair after all? Thistle was right in her observations—the Named were resourceful. The hard part was the decision.

"Why are you asking for this? Is it for Quiet Hunter's sake?"

"He is some of the reason. Not biggest part."

"Then for your sake?"

"Not biggest part either."

"Then what is the biggest part?"

She watched Thistle take a deep breath. "The Dreambiter, Mother."

Puzzled to the point of irritation, Ratha tried to get Thistle to explain what she meant.

"Can't say it any different way," Thistle retorted. "That's how it comes out."

Ratha tried a different approach. "What does your nightmare have to do with saving True-of-voice?"

Thistle's tone sharpened. "Dreambiter is not just mine. Yours too. Don't know what joining part is. Have to dig for it. But there is one. Feel it."

What you mean is that the Dreambiter will soon claim True-of-voice and his people as victims. But I don't have any alternative, Thistle. How can I make you understand?

After Thistle had finished speaking, she left. Ratha thought for a while and then called her people together. She told them what Thistle had asked her to do.

Everybody gave her incredulous looks. Except Thakur. He just looked amazed.

"Are you asking for help in deciding this, clan leader?" Bira asked in her gentle voice.

"I must make the choice," Ratha said. "But hearing what all of you have to say will help me."

"I like Thistle a lot," Bira said, curling her plumed tail about her feet, "so this is hard for me to say. I do not think that her suggestion is a wise one. Perhaps it would be, if she were the only one involved. For us, it is not."

Khushi agreed with Bira. If anything, he was more vehement. "When this enemy leader dies, the hunter tribe will fall apart. There's nothing wrong in letting that happen. Maybe it'll stop them from hurting us. If it doesn't, I'm all for using the Red Tongue." He paused and added, "Why make a weak enemy strong again? It is stupid."

Well-spoken, Fessran's son, thought Ratha, but she felt a twinge of sadness.

And why does Thakur have this strange expression on his face, as if he's been eating rotted fruit?

"Herding teacher, have you thought of something interesting?" she asked mildly.

"Thistle," he said, his voice almost dreamy. "I thought I knew her all the way through. But she's surprised me. She's followed trails that even I have not dared to run."

"None of us can follow *you*, respected Thakur," said Bira. "Please, can you tell us what you mean?"

Thakur sat up a bit straighter and gathered himself together. "I have asked us not to harm these people. But Thistle has gone far beyond me. She has asked us to help them!"

Khushi grimaced. "You think it's wonderful? I think it's crazy! I like her, too, but sometimes I get the feeling that not everything is working between her ears."

"I wouldn't say it quite that strongly," Bira interjected, "but I have to point out that Thistle is asking *us* to take this risk, not her. She is not a clan member; she chose not to be. By that choice, she gave away any right to influence what we do."

"Everything Bira says is true," Thakur said after the Firekeeper had finished speaking. "Remember, though, Thistle came because I asked for her help."

"We can be grateful without doing something that would not be good for us," Bira argued.

Ratha held up a paw for silence. "So it is clear how you all feel. Khushi, you are in favor of using the Red Tongue and not helping the hunters. Bira agrees?"

"Yes, clan leader," said the young Firekeeper. "My loyalty is to you and the rest of us."

"I know how Thakur feels," Ratha said. "All right. I appreciate what you all had to say."

"What about you, Ratha?" Thakur asked.

"I can only tell you how I feel, which won't help. I can't tell you what I will decide."

And the Named left their leader alone, knowing that she needed time to think.

CHAPTER 21

THISTLE WENT BACK to Quiet Hunter, wishing she could do something more for him. He was in a dazed, half-awake state since he had not been able to sleep.

When he lifted his head to touch noses with her, his nose leather was cold, even though he lay in a patch of sun.

For him, everything is icy water, she thought.

She curled around him, trying to drive away the frozen despair.

"Any better?" she asked. "Or everything still cold?"

"Thistle is warm," he said, and his whiskers lifted a little. "But Quiet Hunter is too weary to come out to where Thistle is."

She gave an unhappy sigh. There had to be a way to help him. There *had* to.

But the only thing that could help him was True-of-voice's song. She wished she could become like True-of-voice so that she could help Quiet Hunter.

She grimaced scornfully at herself. She could not begin to do what True-of-voice had done. Wishing was useless. But she still desperately wanted to help Quiet Hunter.

If she tried hard, she could remember how True-of-voice's song sounded and felt, but she couldn't give it to Quiet Hunter. She couldn't reach his "inside ears." Not the way True-of-voice had.

But you have outside ears too, and I have a voice, even if it is a small one, she thought.

"Listen, Quiet Hunter," she said, and let her memory lift her voice as she began to sing softly to him.

Ratha did not stay by herself for long. Hard thinking had dug up a possible solution. It was crazy, but it might work. It might accomplish both objectives without harm to anyone except True-of-voice, and nothing would save him anyway.

To try her idea, she would have to convince Thistle. She felt as though her heart would hammer right through her ribs as she went looking for her daughter.

She didn't find Thistle until she went to the place where she had last seen Quiet Hunter. Her daughter was there. And she was doing something that raised Ratha's hopes even further. Thistle was singing to Quiet Hunter. As she said that True-of-voice had done. Except that Thistle was using her real voice. And the song was no longer without words.

Ratha saw the tortured look in Quiet Hunter's eyes fade. They closed, his head sank down onto his paws, and his sides rose and fell in the rhythm of sleep.

She listened, entranced. Thistle sang more eloquently than she could speak, of the pain and struggle and grief and then of the greening of hope, a slender thread that could bind back together the most broken of spirits. Or lives.

She sang as none of the Named had sung before, blending gifts from both peoples whose trails she had run. Ratha heard it with a shiver that ran down her back and an ache in her belly that could have been grief or joy.

The song was not the strong, certain river that Thistle had described as flowing from True-of-voice. It keened with questions. It wavered with fear. It was the trickle of the spring, not the flow of the river. It was at the same time uplifting and heartbreaking.

And as Ratha watched and listened, she felt that something sacred was happening that she dare not disturb.

Who is she, this one who came from my blood, from my belly? My daughter, chaser of thistles, wayfarer on strange trails.

Who is she?

I know, and yet I do not.

As if sensing the presence of her mother, Thistle, without looking up, brought her song to an end. She crouched down, licked the sleeping Quiet Hunter, and walked forward to greet her mother.

Ratha felt the distance, almost the remoteness of the nose-touch, the whisker-brush. She found it hard to begin speaking, feeling that her words were crude and clumsy after the soaring beauty of Thistle's song.

Yet she had to.

She let Thistle lead her away so that their voices would not wake Quiet Hunter.

"Thistle, I—I think there may be a way out of this.

A way to not hurt anyone. A way to help everyone. Will you listen?"

"Will hear."

"It needs you."

Thistle only cocked her head and widened her eyes in the same way as Ratha knew that she herself did. It was unsettling to see herself reflected in her daughter.

Never had Ratha struggled so to speak, and she felt for an instant a deeper sympathy for Thistle's struggle with language than she had ever felt before.

Finally she said, "It needs you to sing to the hunters. The same way you did to your friend. To keep them from going wild and attacking us."

Thistle's eyes only grew a little wider.

"Thistle, I'm asking you to go back to the hunters. Make it easier for them to accept True-of-voice's death. I know that it is dangerous, but if you give them what they need, they won't hurt you."

Her daughter's words came slowly. "Asking me . . . to replace True-of-voice?"

Ratha was about to protest that the two things were not the same, but the look in her daughter's eyes kept her silent. "Yes," she admitted. "I guess that is what I am asking."

"You want . . . me . . . to lead the hunters. To keep them happy so that you Named . . . can take face-tails . . . without fighting."

"Yes." Ratha watched for the first sign of outrage or anger, but Thistle remained calm. "It is the only way to keep either side from suffering. Can't you see?"

Thistle gave a strange snort and then started shaking

all over, her mouth open, as if yawning. "You Named ones. You are so arrogant . . . that it's . . . funny. You really think . . . me being a True-of-voice . . . makes all problems go away?"

"Why shouldn't it work?" Ratha felt herself bristling.

Thistle only opened her mouth in another strange, soundless gape.

"If you only understood. . . ."

"Then make me understand," Ratha challenged. "Why can't you sing to the hunters, keep them from despairing, going wild, dying . . . ? You care about Quiet Hunter's people. Isn't it up to you to save them?"

Thistle stopped shaking and gaping. Ratha felt a sudden chill at the despairing look that came into Thistle's sea-colored eyes. "Cannot do what True-of-voice does. Not even enough to save Quiet Hunter."

"I thought . . ."

"He is dying. Sing to make it less frightening. Is all I can do."

"Then . . ." Ratha stumbled.

"Only way to save them is to save True-of-voice. Brook dries up without a spring to feed it. Same for them." Thistle paused. "Not up to me to save Quiet Hunter and his people, Mother. Is up to you."

Questions. All she can give me is questions. I have to find my own answers.

Ratha walked alone. No one could help her with the challenge she faced now. Not Thakur. Not Bira. Not even Thistle herself.

The Dreambiter. Why is she still talking about the Dreambiter? I thought she had come to terms with it.

And then Ratha knew why Thistle had spoken earlier about the Dreambiter.

It is still here. It is still prowling. Wearing my skin, my whiskers, my fur.

No, all I want is for my people to survive. That is all I have ever wanted.

Is that the truth, Ratha?

What is it that raised the torch against the Un-Named, killed the old clan leader Meoran, brought down Shong-shar, caused Bonechewer's death? I cared for him more deeply than anyone I had ever known. I nearly killed Thistle. I certainly changed her.

Who is the Dreambiter, Ratha?

The part that hates. That fears. That wants to kill.

No. All I wanted was to see my people survive.

And then, as if from a distance, she seemed to hear Thakur's voice saying, "Why can't there be room in the world for the Named and others too? Why must things that help the Named harm others?"

The hunters aren't like us. They are alien. They are wrong. It is too hard to understand them. Easier to push them out of the way. Save True-of-voice? A tyrant worse than Meoran or Shongshar? Who not only commands their bodies, but their every thought?

Rescue True-of-voice. Make his people what they were. The Named would think I was no longer fit to be leader. They'd throw me out. Can't you understand that, Thistle?

She should understand. She's been hurt enough.

Is she crazy? Is she right?

I am shaking. I am afraid. Of what?

The shadows that run through my mind. The shadows that bite and tear, that kill and maim what I love. I put words on them. "Un-Named ones." "Enemies." "Not like us." "Wrong." "Alien." "Deserve to die."

Many shadows, and they are all Dreambiters, Dreamkillers. They all blend into one. It prowls, hurting.

No one deserves to die except the Dreambiter. No one deserves to be cast out except the Dreambiter. No one deserves to lie bleeding, in pain. Even if they are different. Even if you do not understand how they think. Even if you think they might hurt you.

The question comes again.

Who is the Dreambiter, Ratha?

I know now, Thistle. I know.

Quiet Hunter was asleep. Thistle did not need to sing to him any longer. Yet she stayed by him, knowing that if he did wake, he would need her.

She thought about Ratha. What her mother had suggested was ridiculous. It showed that Ratha had only a very shallow idea of what was going on. No one could replace True-of-voice among the hunters. The idea that she, Thistle, who was in some ways marginal even among the Named, could take the place of the wellspring of the song, had gone beyond the ridiculous to the tragic.

No one could replace True-of-voice except another of his blood and breed. For various reasons, that other had not yet been birthed.

Yes, that was a fault in the society of the hunters. But it would not have been so fatal had not the Named intervened.

Was part of that as well. Did not mean to be, Thistle thought, looking down at Quiet Hunter.

Asleep, the young male looked like any of the Named. He looked a bit like Thakur, in some ways, though his eyes and coat were a different color. A certain gentleness, a certain curiosity about life, a certain willingness to explore, had perhaps not only shaped his character, but sculpted the lines of his face.

No. See traces of Thakur in Quiet Hunter because I want them to be there.

She wondered if perhaps her thoughts had been drawn to Thakur because she was getting the herding teacher's scent on the breeze. As it grew stronger, her hopes leaped up. Perhaps Thakur was coming.

She lifted her muzzle as a familiar pattern of footfalls added itself to the herding teacher's scent. And then Thakur padded forward and lay down with Thistle and Quiet Hunter.

He said little, but his presence, his solid warmth, and, above all, the sense of his wisdom helped ease Thistle's tension.

"Can talk, Thakur. Quiet Hunter is so asleep . . . won't hear." She paused. "Don't think he is really sleeping anymore. Has gone down deeper than that. To escape the world both inside and outside."

"I am sorry, Thistle," Thakur said. "I tried to help him, but my skills are not enough."

"Tried to help, too. Tried to bring him into my world. But he said things were too clear, too sharp. Knowing there was only one behind the eyes . . . too lonely." She paused. "Know what he feels. Hurt me, too, when song went away. But being one behind the eyes . . . have always known it. And all of you Named ones know it, too."

She felt Thakur's tongue on the ragged ruff that was starting to grow around her neck.

"Sometimes being one behind the eyes hurts us, Thistle," he said softly. "Maybe we are closer to Quiet Hunter's people than we think."

Thistle laid her chin on her paws briefly before she spoke again. "My mother. Seen her yet?"

"Not for a while. She went off by herself to think."

Thistle stared ahead at nothing. "Don't know if she can make the jump I am asking her to make. Remember all the times she couldn't. Wish I could hope, Thakur, but don't dare."

"Thistle, it is hard for her. Do you know that she is not a great deal older than you?"

"Than me? But mothers . . . fathers, always seem so much older. Seems hard to believe."

"I know."

"Not a lot older than me," Thistle mused. "Still learning." She turned her gaze to him. "Thakur, can . . . I . . . dare hope? Not expect. Hope."

"Yes," he said. "Yes, I think you can."

I see them both together as I come near. The two who demand the most of me. Thistle and Thakur. Do I see disappointment in their eyes even before I tell them what I will do?

Thakur knows this is not easy. Thistle . . . She thinks anything is possible for the Named. Anything except looking beyond the needs of your own people.

But seeing first to the needs of your own people is what a good leader does, isn't it?

Not always.

What helps the Named does not have to harm others. Not when you can see them without the shadow of the Dreambiter darkening their shapes.

I am taking the leap, daughter of mine. Help me land safely on the far edge.

As Ratha finished speaking to Thakur and Thistle, she watched the shock in her daughter's eyes turn first to amazement . . . then to joy. Then she was nearly knocked off her feet by Thistle's boisterous rubbing, purring, and licking.

"Wait!" she protested as her daughter sprang around in happiness. "I've only said that I will help rescue True-of-voice if we can find a way. I haven't *found* that way yet."

But Thistle, in her triumph and joy, seemed to think that the hardest part of the task was over.

Perhaps it was.

The camp of the Named was in an uproar. Ratha had a hard time calming everyone down after her announcement. She had expected that it would be Fessran's son, Khushi, who would be hardest to convince, but instead it was Bira.

"I am not asking you to agree with me," Ratha said finally, when the gentle but stubborn little Firekeeper refused to give up ground. "As clan leader, I don't need agreement, even if I would like it. What I need is help."

"Help in doing something that might hurt us?" Bira asked. "Ratha, I want to trust you, but this trail looks so treacherous."

"I know how treacherous it feels. I've been on it. Bira, there is a chance that rescuing True-of-voice may hurt us. I'm ready to accept the blame if it does. But I feel now that there is a greater chance that it will help us as well as the hunters." Ratha paused. "If you really can't live with this, you can return to the seacoast with your treeling, if you want."

"No. You need a Firekeeper," Bira said staunchly as her treeling, Biaree, groomed her ruff. "I will stand behind you, clan leader."

Standing in the center of the circle, looking at those gathered about her, Ratha at once felt immense pride and humility.

The pride was for her people as well as herself. There they were, around her. She was their center, and they her support. They had put aside personal reservations to do what their leader thought right.

Impulsive, sometimes foolish, but always well-intentioned Khushi. Bira—dainty, calm, her gentleness covering a deep-seated stubbornness that was only exceeded by her loyalty. Thakur, teacher of healing, herding, and living life in the most honest way. He was the essence and spirit of the Named.

And now Thistle, with her strange mixture of gifts and deficits. Of all, she was the unexpected visionary. She who had been most deeply wounded was perhaps the strongest among them. If she does not lead the Named, she will guide them, Ratha thought, and had a strong sense that she was looking at the future of her people embodied in her daughter.

No. She will serve more than the Named. Quiet Hunter and his people may be only the start. And I hope that I may be able to reach far enough beyond my limitations to help her.

"Well," said Khushi, after the discussion had finally died down. "Now that we've decided what to do, we'd better figure out how to do it. True-of-voice probably doesn't have much life left."

Nor does Quiet Hunter, Ratha thought as she saw Thistle glancing at a shape lying still beneath the trees.

When Thistle felt that she could spend a few moments away from Quiet Hunter, she went to her mother and the others of the Named, who had gathered to figure out a way to save True-of-voice.

"We all saw the cliff," Ratha was saying as Thistle joined the group. "Does anyone remember seeing any way to reach the ledge he's on?"

"Maybe we should go and look again," Khushi suggested.

"I wish we could," Ratha said, "but the hunters are pretty stirred up. If we try, they'll attack."

"Then how are we going to get close enough to rescue True-of-voice?" Khushi asked, his voice doubtful.

Thistle was startled when the Firekeeper Bira turned to her and said, "You were with the hunters for a long time at the top of the cliff. Did you see any way down to the ledge?"

She replayed the scene over in her mind as she had

done countless times. She had peered over the edge until her eyes ached, searching for a path down to the trapped leader. There was a slanting, rocky shelf that descended partway, but it petered out before it reached the larger ledge where True-of-voice was.

"Could only get halfway there," Thistle said, and was about to add that it wouldn't do any good when her gaze fell on Biaree, Bira's treeling. Those creatures were good at climbing. At least in trees.

Bira inclined her head and gazed down at her treeling, who was grooming the ruff around her neck. Thistle watched the expression in Bira's eyes change, and could almost follow her thoughts. First came astonishment, then recognition of a new possibility, but after that was a touch of fear and defensiveness.

Ratha was not slow to pick up the meaning of Thistle's look and Bira's response. Thistle could see her mother was trying to decide if this idea was quarry worth chasing.

"You think that Biaree could climb down the cliff to True-of-voice," Ratha said.

"Treeling is smaller. Lighter. More toes to use for holding on," Thistle answered.

"Even if Biaree could reach the ledge, what could he do?" This was from Khushi, who looked more skeptical than ever.

The reply, to Thistle's surprise, came from Bira. "He could do a lot, Khushi. He could take bits of meat and melon down to the trapped leader. True-of-voice is probably dying of hunger and thirst as well as his injuries." Her voice faded slightly as she looked down again at Biaree, and Thistle felt a stab of remorse.

"Don't want treeling to get hurt," she stammered. "Know how much you care for him, Bira. Maybe . . . too much to ask?"

"I think it is a good idea, Thistle," Bira answered slowly.

"I wish it wasn't so risky for Biaree," Ratha said. "If I had brought Ratharee or Thakur had his treeling . . ."

Thakur, who had just been listening up to this point, made a suggestion. "Bira, I've seen you and Biaree bundle up twigs with lengths of vine. Biaree knows how to tie things. If you could get a very long length and get him to tie it around his middle and someone held onto it, he couldn't fall."

Thistle felt her ears prick up. How clever Thakur was! To see something that the Named used every day and be able to turn it to another purpose . . . that was a gift indeed.

She found herself making pictures in her mind. Of how the vine would attach to the treeling by using the controlled tangle that the Named called a "knot." Of how the vine would run from the treeling to someone else who held the end in their jaws.

"Even if we can reach True-of-voice, and feed him to keep him alive, we haven't solved the problem," Ratha pointed out. "How are we going to get him *down*?"

And then the pictures in Thistle's mind changed. Instead of seeing the vine tied to the treeling, the vine was tied to True-of-voice. And all of the Named were pulling, to lift the injured hunter up the cliff.

But would the vine be strong enough? For a treeling, yes, but not for True-of-voice.

"Would break," Thistle muttered.

"What would break?" Ratha asked, and her gaze became sharp.

"Vines."

"Vines?"

"The ones tied to True-of-voice," Thistle said, wishing she had kept her silly thoughts to herself.

"How do they get tied onto him?"

"Treeling. If he can."

Everyone sat staring at her. Thistle felt as though she wanted to slink away, back to Quiet Hunter. It was a stupid idea. True-of-voice was too heavy to be pulled up by vines. They would break. There was no point in risking Bira's treeling for something that would never work.

But Bira herself was looking back with widened eyes. "I think you've got something, Thistle."

Thakur and Ratha agreed.

"But couldn't pull him up," Thistle said. "Vines would rub on edge of cliff and break. He too heavy, even for all of us together."

"We might not be able to pull him up," Thakur said. "Once we got him off the ledge, however, we could lower him."

The hopeful expression on his face began to spread to the others. Thistle felt it bubble up inside her. She looked to her mother and saw that the same hope was lighting Ratha's eyes.

And not only hope. Pride as well. "I think it will be tricky, but it will work," she heard Ratha say.

"Three yowls for Thistle," Khushi crowed, and followed it up with earsplitting praise.

The meeting dissolved in a hubbub as the Named made their plans and assigned tasks. Thakur and Khushi set out to scout the forest for the heaviest vines they could find. Bira found a length of jungle creeper and began the task of teaching Biaree to attach it around his middle. Using Ratha and Thistle as models, she also had the treeling tie short lengths of vine around their paws.

"There is only one problem," Bira said to Thistle, as she nudged the treeling into looping a length of vine about one of Thistle's forepaws.

"What?" asked Ratha, who was watching.

"I can send Biaree down with food or melon bits for True-of-voice. That's not such a complicated thing. But tying vines onto someone's paws, especially if Biaree doesn't know that someone—that may be the hard part."

"He won't do it?" Ratha asked as Thistle felt her hopes sag.

"He will, but I'll have to go down with him at least partway to coax him. I'm willing to try," Bira added. "Thistle said there was a slanting shelf on the face."

Thistle watched the way her mother looked at Bira. "That shelf is pretty narrow. I saw it. Even the treeling is going to have a hard time."

Bira looked steadily back at Ratha. In the Firekeeper's gaze, Thistle saw the words that Bira did not need to say. *Even if I risk falling, I'll try it.*

The clan's deep loyalty to Ratha, despite her mistakes, made Thistle feel envious for a moment. It also brought a new respect for her mother.

"Could Biaree work with someone other than you?" Ratha asked Bira.

Bira looked startled. "Why yes, clan leader. But why?"

"Because I can't let you risk your life as well as your treeling," Ratha said. "And I won't."

"Don't worry about me, clan leader. The important thing is doing what needs to be done, which is saving True-of-voice." Bira's voice sounded calm, but Thistle picked up a slight tremor underneath.

"I am the one who made the decision to attempt the rescue," Ratha said. "I won't ask any of you to take the risk. Unless I fail."

"But clan leader," Bira faltered, and then fell silent.

Thistle felt a bolt of fear go through her. Fear for her mother. That Ratha might die in a fall from the cliff, leaving the Named leaderless. And herself without Ratha, just as she was really starting to know her mother.

"None of you can go," Thistle heard herself say sharply. "All too . . . big!"

There was a silence. Ratha glowered, while Bira looked thoughtful. "She has a point," the Firekeeper said.

Ratha's answer was a low growl. "I know. I wish she didn't."

Thistle interrupted. "Better chance for me. Smaller. Lighter. Not part of clan. Not needed. Or not as much as you and Bira."

"Face-tail dung!" Ratha exploded. "Of all the idiot things to say! Thakur needed you enough to bring you here. And if you think I'm going to let you hang your scrawny tail over the cliff—what if you get one of those fits?"

Thistle shivered inside at the thought of being attacked

by her illness, but she refused to back down. "My problem," she said, thrusting her nose forward until her muzzle nearly met Ratha's. "Not yours. Not clan member . . . don't have to obey you. Can do as I want . . . hang tail where you can't get to . . . can do what you can't!"

"Thistle . . ."

"No, listen, my mother and clan leader. You chose to help hunters. But who pushed you . . . nagged you . . . made you think? Not any Named!"

With a thrill, Thistle realized that she was actually pushing against Ratha's nose. She, the little half-Named scruffball, was making the clan leader give ground.

"Am going to take my scrawny tail down the cliff to True-of-voice. Only way to stop me is to say I can't use Bira's treeling."

Ratha was going back on her haunches, but Thistle didn't stop her advance. Not while she had her newly beloved foe on the run. "You going to do that? Tell Bira to not let me use treeling? Throw away one *real* chance to save True-of-voice?"

Abruptly, Thistle jerked her head away from Ratha's nose. "Am going. With or without treeling." She started to pace away.

There was utter silence behind her.

All right, they were going to make things hard. She was used to dealing with things when they were hard. Including her mother.

And then came a roar that made her ears flatten.

"Thistle-chaser, come back here or I'll—"

She turned around, lifted her tail and her chin.

"—have to *bring* you the treeling!"

CHAPTER 22

THE FOLLOWING MORNING, everyone in Ratha's group assembled at the foot of the trail up to the cliff top. To Thistle's surprise, Quiet Hunter was there, too, even though he looked weak and shaky.

"Must tell people that you are trying to help," he said, leaning against Thakur, who stood beside him. Thistle felt a strong surge of affection and gratitude to the herding teacher for his dedication to Quiet Hunter. Thakur had stayed beside him, trying to calm him, to heal the pain caused by the loss of the song. Even though the gentle healer and teacher knew that his caring would not save Quiet Hunter, he gave all that he could.

And now Quiet Hunter, in his own way, was trying to give something back.

Thistle was startled by something touching the nape of her neck. It was the treeling, a still-strange sensation. She wasn't used to carrying Biaree, although he had been with her since the end of the teaching sessions of the previous day. Bira had insisted on this, though Thistle knew that the Firekeeper missed the companionship of her treeling.

One day and one night—it wasn't nearly enough time

to form the kind of partnership that the task demanded. If not ready, my fault, not Biaree's, Thistle thought. For it was as if the treeling understood the importance of what he was being trained to do. He had accepted both an abrupt change in companions as well as an intense series of training sessions. And all without any treeling fussiness or outbursts of temper.

He had tied innumerable knots around Named paws with various different sizes of vines. Thakur, in addition to caring for Quiet Hunter, had doubled as paw donor, for his feet were probably the closest in size to True-of-voice's. He had to put up not only with having loops tied around his feet but with having the vines yanked on, since Biaree had been taught to test knots as well as make them.

Now the Named were about to see if all their preparation was enough.

Thistle watched as Ratha arranged everyone for the climb up the trail and the first confrontation with the hunters who were still keeping vigil for True-of-voice. She felt herself fidgeting with impatience as Ratha trotted from one to the other, assigning them their roles in the rescue attempt. She had sought True-of-voice's song and could not find it. The leader might already be dead, or close to it. Any more delay and . . .

Even so, Thistle could see that what her mother was doing made sense. Ratha had put herself, Khushi, and Bira in the lead. Bira carried fire embers, nestled in a sand-filled basket that had a carrying loop. She and her treeling had made it together. Khushi had a mouthful of dry pine branches that would light quickly, if needed. It was a compromise—Ratha had originally wanted Bira to carry a lighted torch to repel any attack. It was not Thistle's objection that had changed the clan leader's mind, but Quiet Hunter's soft plea that the Red Tongue not be used against his people unless there was no other way.

Thistle herself was next, with Biaree on her shoulders. Behind her came Thakur, with loops and coils of heavy vines tied onto his back and flanks. He also had a few packets of food and chunks of melon, so that the hunger and thirst that threatened True-of-voice might be fended off long enough to get the trapped leader down. Beside Thakur walked Quiet Hunter, carrying some of the lighter coils of vine ropes.

"All right, Thistle," Ratha announced. "We're ready."

Ratha and Bira set the upward pace—a ground-eating jog-trot. Even so, Thistle had to keep herself from forcing her way forward or crowding the three before her. She also fought to control her fear that True-of-voice might be beyond help. She needed to keep calm in order to avoid alarming Biaree. So far the partnership had worked out astonishingly well, but she knew how quickly it had been formed and how easily it might be destroyed.

It was hard going, especially the last section of the trail, which led to the top, where the hunters were still gathered. Thistle felt herself sweating so heavily through her pads that dust seemed to turn to slippery mud beneath her feet. Would the hunters attack? Would they rush the party as soon as she and the Named appeared? If she were attacked, what would Biaree do? Could they keep the treeling safe from the hunters?

Can't lose Biaree. WIthout him, have no hope of rescuing True-of-voice.

Thistle watched Khushi, trotting ahead of her, clench his teeth on the unlit firebrands as the party emerged from the trail to the cliff top.

"Slow," came Ratha's voice from in front, and everyone eased to a cautious pace. Thistle could feel Biaree crouch down low on her neck. She gave a low purr to reassure him, the way Bira had taught her.

Now she could see the hunters. They were still gathered at the cliff edge. Some were sprawled out the way Quiet Hunter had been until she sang to him. Some were staggering back and forth, their bleeding paws mute witness that they had been pacing like this for days. Some were circling endlessly, their heads hanging low.

None had groomed or eaten, despite the presence of meat from the kill lying in rotting, fly-ridden piles. Their coats were dusty, matted. Some of the hunters had bare, raw patches where they had obsessively licked themselves or pulled out hair. Ribs showed and stomachs were shrunken. Drool hung from half-open mouths.

Thistle felt her own belly clench at the sight. Thought I was exaggerating about them dying. But they are.

She hoped that the hunters might be too weak or crazed to offer the Named any resistance, but her hope faded as the mourning howls turned to snarls, heads were lowered, and teeth showed.

In front, she saw Ratha narrow her eyes, take an unlit firebrand from Khushi, and hold it, ready to dip the end in Bira's embers. There was suddenly a flurry behind

her as Quiet Hunter staggered forward as fast as his
shaky legs would carry him. Past the Firekeeper, past
the clan leader, out to his own people, even though they
had expelled him, threatened to kill him . . .

Looking at the torture in their eyes, Thistle knew that
loss and pain were demanding blood, and they did not
care whose. And looking at her mother's face and the
jaws gripping the torch, she knew that Ratha was ready
to defend her own group—and Quiet Hunter—with the
equal savagery of the Red Tongue.

Hoping that Biaree would stay quiet, Thistle also left
her place, moving toward her mother. She heard Quiet
Hunter speaking, trying to fend off the threatened attack
with gentle words. He knew their pain, he said. He,
too, was dying from it. But the ones with him intended
to help. They had not come to prey but to heal.

The hunters would not believe. They were too deeply
in pain to believe. The sight and smell of the strangers
and the hint of their weapon, even though hidden in the
basket of sand and embers, was too much to accept.
Thistle knew that things would break down—were already breaking down, even though Quiet Hunter was
desperately trying to get through to the rest.

"Quiet Hunter offers himself," she heard him saying.
"If anger must take life, then Quiet Hunter is ready. If
the pain of losing the song is eased by killing, then Quiet
Hunter is willing to be killed."

His words sent a charge of fear through Thistle, so
strongly that she felt the treeling react, too—hunching
and stiffening. It was all she could do not to leap to
Quiet Hunter's side with teeth bared and claws ready.
But she knew that if she did, both he and she would

die, and the treeling as well. Even scaring Biaree might destroy any chance of saving True-of-voice.

As she purred to quiet the treeling, she saw Ratha turn her head, the torch-stick in her mouth moving to the source that birthed the Red Tongue.

If the flame-creature took life at the end of the branch, Quiet Hunter would not die, but any chance of reaching the hunters would. Though Thistle's whole being cried out in agony at the choice, she made it.

With a quick nudge, Thistle sent Biaree to temporary safety with Bira.

Moving more quickly and quietly than she thought she could, she reached Ratha. Her teeth met around the unlit torch in Ratha's mouth. As her eyes met those of her mother, she felt Ratha resist, and the branch was held between them in an abrupt tugging contest.

Ratha flicked her gaze toward Quiet Hunter, who stood with head lowered, accepting the claw swipes that were already opening wounds on his sides and flanks. His refusal to defend or guard himself was making the attackers hesitate, but it wouldn't keep them off for long.

"For him," Thistle heard her mother hiss through her teeth.

For an instant they were locked together, braced against each other. Thistle knew that her mother was stronger. Ratha could jerk the firebrand away from her easily. Yet something seemed to be happening deep in her green eyes. Ratha's jaws loosened on the unlit firebrand, and Thistle heard the whisper of her mother's voice. "For you, Thistle."

The stick was in her own mouth and her heart was

pounding wildly. She threw it aside. It was not the weapon to defend Quiet Hunter. But what was?

And then she heard it—the distant, slender echo in her mind. The song. And it said, This One knows what Thistle-chaser is trying to do. If only the people would understand.

They would if they could hear you, True-of-voice.

Then let them hear. Through you. Sing to them.

My song, my voice—not the same. Cannot be the same for them. They need the center, the soul, the strength.

The strength is gone. Death is too near. From True-of-voice take the center and the soul. From you, add the strength.

Thistle couldn't answer. She could make no reply. Only to search within herself for what he asked for.

And then, as Quiet Hunter reeled back from another vicious strike and the threatening snarls from the hunters grew deeper, Thistle lifted her voice in the song.

Ratha looked up at the sky. The sun had moved only a little, but somehow things below—in hearts, bellies, and heads—had moved an immense distance.

She glanced at Quiet Hunter, who was with his people. The one who had first struck him was now licking and soothing his wounds. Such was the power of the song, even when it came from Thistle.

I'll never understand these hunters, she thought. I'll probably never like them, but at least I'm willing to give them a chance.

She crouched by the cliff edge, watching Thistle send

Biaree down with bits of food and thirst-quenching melon for True-of-voice. Thakur had said that hunger and thirst were probably weakening him more than any injuries he might have. The hunters lay as close as they could get, yet out of the way of the rescue effort.

Thakur crouched close to Thistle so that Biaree could take the bits of life-preserving food to the one who so desperately needed them. In his mouth Thakur held the end of the slender vine safety rope. The other end was knotted securely about the treeling's middle. Bira and Khushi stood ready to help Thakur with the rope or get more food.

Biaree had already made several trips up and down the cliff face, carrying as much as he could, but to Ratha, the amounts seemed woefully small.

She joined the rescuers, settling beside Thakur.

"I think we've fed True-of-voice as much as we can," the herding teacher was saying to Thistle. "We don't want to tire Biaree out; he's still got to get the vines tied onto the leader's paws and around his chest, if possible."

Ratha felt a growing apprehension. Soon would come the moment that she dreaded, when Thistle would descend with her borrowed treeling. She felt that she had too many things to say, yet could not say any of them. She wished deeply that she could be the one to act in Thistle's place, but she knew that she couldn't. All other considerations aside, there was the simple fact that Thistle was the smallest of the party and better able to sidle along the narrow shelf. She, like the treeling, would have a safety line, and her lighter weight would minimize the chances of it snapping.

Although a good jerk probably would break it, Ratha thought. We don't know. We haven't been able to try it out. I wouldn't be so worried if it weren't for those wretched fits. They attack her at the worst possible times.

She listened as Thakur and her daughter talked about the difficulties Biaree would encounter when the treeling went down with the ropes. If True-of-voice was awake, he might be able to help by lifting his limbs and other parts so that Biaree could pass the vine rope around them. Yet, if he was awake, he might accidentally scare the treeling, especially if he was in delirium or only half-conscious.

"Can you reach him?" Thakur asked.

"Difficult. Not clear. Fading in and out." Thistle squeezed her eyes shut. "Can't be sure. Really reached him? Don't know. Maybe song voices were all in my own head."

"Well, even if they were, they were the right voices."

"So strange," Thistle said. "Even for me." She shook herself. "Can't wait any longer. Treeling Biaree," she said, gently nudging her borrowed companion, "True-of-voice won't hurt you. Go now. Quickly."

She looked deeply into the treeling's sharp black eyes, making Ratha wonder if the strange gift that made Thistle able to speak to True-of-voice's people also worked with treelings. And then with a chitter and a scamper, the treeling was down on the cliff face, finding his way to the trapped leader, holding the end of the vine rope alternately in his teeth or wound around with his tail.

Thistle wore a vine-rope harness made of two loops.

One ran under her chest behind her forelegs; the other was a breastband that anchored the first. Thakur had suggested it and Biaree had tied it, under Bira's direction. Biaree had also tied the far end to a stout spur of rock. It would help in case of a fall, but it was no guarantee.

Ratha, wrapped up in her thoughts, was startled when Thistle's cool nose leather touched her own.

"Be with me," said the soft yet strong voice. "In heart, in breath. Even in guts."

"I will be, especially the guts," said Ratha, for she felt her own start to roll and twist with trepidation. She forced herself to watch as Thistle started to climb down, headfirst, after the treeling.

Keep eyes fixed on True-of-voice. Don't look beyond. Too far down. No, don't think about down. There is no down. Just True-of-voice, looking dead.

No, he can't be. Not after all this. True-of-voice, you aren't dead, are you?

Can't reach him now. Have to think too hard. Where to put each foot. How hard to drive in each claw.

Pads are sweaty. Have to stop, wipe carefully on fur. More sweat.

Biaree, don't get too far ahead. Know you are impatient. Don't blame you. Want to get this over as fast as possible, but sweaty pads make it slow.

Prrrp. Calling him, just like Bira taught me. *Prrrp!* Yes, he's obeying. Good treeling. Wait for Thistle.

Flank against the rock. . . . Heart banging. Feels like it is trying to beat me right off this slab of rock.

No, don't think about that. Just keep paws moving or they'll freeze. True-of-voice, don't be dead. Please don't be dead.

Stupid, Thistle. He is alive or he isn't. Wishing doesn't make any difference.

If only it wasn't so far to reach him. . . .

Slow, hard, with damp paw pads. Wish I had a tail that could curl around things the way Biaree's does.

Biaree, you are nearly there. Move slowly, carefully. Don't be frightened. *Prrrr.* Good treeling, clever treeling. Tie the rope.

Arrr! True-of-voice moved. Don't skitter away, Biaree. He won't hurt you. He's trying to help by lifting his paw.

Biaree's fur is fluffed. True-of-voice moved too fast. Startled Biaree. Please, treeling, please go back.

He looks at me. Wants me down with him. Doesn't have the courage to touch True-of-voice again unless I'm there.

Can't . . . get there! Shelf narrows to nothing.

Biaree, please.

No good. Got scared. Doesn't trust.

Face-tail dung! Everything ruined because True-of-voice twitched.

Biaree won't go if I'm not down there to encourage him.

Won't give up. Won't!

I'm coming even if I have to find clawholds on the bare rock.

Prrrp! I'm coming, Biaree. Banging heart, scrawny tail, and everything.

* * *

Ratha crouched at the top of the cliff, looking down on Thistle. Her breath came fast and felt like the Red Tongue searing her throat.

Beside her was Thakur, and she could tell from the rigidity of his muscles and the stiffness of his neck that he was nearly as tense.

Both of them had some bad moments when Thistle left the small shelf she was inching along and began to descend, head down, along the open rock face.

Ratha could hardly bear to watch, knowing that at any instant her daughter might lose her hold and go plunging to a terrible death. The safety rope was too thin to stop such a fall. But Thistle had stuck to the cliff face like a tick to skin. Long enough for Biaree to tie vine cord to all four of True-of-voice's limbs. Long enough to cajole and encourage the treeling to actually work a heavy vine rope under True-of-voice's belly and then loop it across the leader's chest, to make a heavier version of the harness that Thistle wore.

She had actually been able to do more than Ratha had hoped for. There was a good chance that the Named could get him down without worsening any of his injuries.

"There. Biaree's coming back to her," Ratha said, letting out a sigh of relief. "They're done, and it looks like all the ropes will hold."

"That's good, since we don't have any more heavy vines," Thakur said.

Ratha glanced sideways, to where Quiet Hunter was trying to explain to his people what the Named were doing. Some of them had come to the cliff edge and peered over. They retreated again, but a more hopeful look had replaced the despair in their faces.

I hope he can persuade a few of them to help when we start lowering True-of-voice. He's no lightweight.

She peered down over the cliff at her daughter. Thistle was still hanging, head down, near True-of-voice. Bi-aree had returned to her. Ratha waited, expecting to see Thistle turn around and climb back up. But she didn't.

A cold feeling started creeping along Ratha's back. Something was going wrong.

Thistle, your part is over. Come back up before you make me wild with worry.

Thakur was also peering over, his eyes narrowed, his whiskers drawn back. "She's in trouble," he hissed. "She can't turn around. She tried and nearly lost her hold. And her tail is shaking."

Ratha's own tail was lashing. Thistle had gotten through the hard part. Why was she faltering now?

You've saved True-of-voice. Now save yourself.

But as Ratha watched, it became ominously clear that Thistle couldn't.

"It's one of her fits," she growled. "At the worst possible time. Thakur, we've got to do something. Can she get down to the ledge where True-of-voice is? Or can we lower her all the way by her harness?"

"There's no room left on the ledge," Thakur answered. "And we don't know if the harness would hold, especially if she jerked it. I'm afraid those vines will snap. And the rope isn't long enough to lower her all the way. I gave her a shorter one, since I assumed that she would be climbing back up."

"Can she take one of the vines off True-of-voice?"

"That would lower our chances of getting him down, Ratha. And I don't think Thistle can do anything right now. You know how the fits affect her." He paused. "Someone is going to have to go down to her. I'll do it, since I should have made her rope longer."

He started to get up, but she put a paw on his back. "There aren't any ropes left, Thakur," she said, trying to speak calmly despite the fear that was rushing through her. "No time to make new ones."

His gaze as he looked into her eyes supplied the answer. *I know. I'm still willing.*

"No," she said. "You can't be the one. I must be."

"Ratha . . ."

"It has nothing to do with who is more valuable to the clan."

"But . . ."

"You've tried to make me understand all along. Now I do. She's *my* daughter, Thakur. That is what matters."

She could see the mixture of emotions in his eyes, but all he said as his nose leather touched hers was, "Go to her, Ratha. We will all be with you."

Thought . . . it would be easy. Thought . . . that the hard part was over.

It is. Biaree has done what he needed to do. Ropes are on True-of-voice. The Named can lower him to safe ground.

Maybe that's why the Dreambiter waited. But now, it is coming.

Climb back down to True-of-voice, treeling. You'll

be safe with him. Not with me. Not with me, hanging by my claws while the Dreambiter prowls.

Tried to do too much too fast. Strained my leg. Hurts. The Dreambiter knows that hurt. That's why it woke. That's why it is coming.

Am shaking. Vision closing. Can't see outside anymore.

At least what I had to do is done.

Dreambiter, you won't endanger anyone else if you take me now.

Shaking. Can barely feel my feet, my claws.

Feel like I am already falling.

Maybe I am.

Waves of white terror washed through Ratha as she sidled along the rock shelf, balancing herself with her long tail. She could see Thistle's footsteps ahead of her in the fine, gritty dirt. They were damp. She knew why. Her own paw pads were slick with sweat.

Each step was harder than the one before, since the shelf was fading back into the cliff face. Ever so carefully she eased herself along, testing every step to be sure the rocks would not crumble away beneath her weight.

Fear came in stabs, each one driving deep, then withdrawing in a wake of sick dizziness. Yet the urge that drove her on overrode everything, and she had to fight not to launch herself in a bold but fatal scramble down the face to where her daughter was clinging.

The ropes running down to True-of-voice were there beside her, but Ratha dared not use them. A scratch or bite might start them fraying or cracking. The ropes had to stay strong—for True-of-voice and his people.

When the moment came to leave the vanishing shelf and climb down headfirst, as Thistle had done, Ratha thought she couldn't. Dread locked up her limbs, froze her will. She could hardly bend her neck to look down.

You have to. Look at Thistle. Keep centered on her. You have to reach her soon or she will fall.

Ratha forced her head down, fixed her gaze on Thistle. She fought a whirlwind that seemed to howl around her, shrieking and moaning in her ears and buffeting her dangerously back and forth. She forced her forelimbs to reach down below the shelf, groping for clawholds.

But the vortex was nearly too much for her, threatening to spin her right off the shelf. She knew what the whirlwind was. It was her body trying to say that this was madness; common sense was trying to take over and send her scrambling back up to a part of the ledge where she would be safe.

Every time she tried to defeat the wildly spinning wind of fear, she was overwhelmed. It was tearing Thistle from her and threatening to destroy both of them.

She heard Thistle cry out and she heard a name she knew well. The Dreambiter had waited long for a chance to attack. Thistle would never be as vulnerable as she was now. And this time, the apparition might claim two victims.

Ratha bared her teeth, flattened her ears. No. The Dreambiter would not win. There was one thing that could slice through the whirlwind of fear: the enemy—hatred for her enemy.

Following the marks of Thistle's clawholds, Ratha climbed down off the rocky shelf. The dread was still there, but it had somehow become remote. The fear-wind was still spinning, but now she had moved into the eye, the center, where the air was still.

And in the center, although distant, as if seen from far down a tunnel, was Thistle. Ratha fixed her gaze on Thistle and let her body take her to her daughter. Her legs somehow knew where to reach, her claws knew how deep to drive, and she trusted in that wisdom.

Suddenly she was beside Thistle, both now hanging head down on the cliff face. Thistle was losing the claw-hold of one forefoot, for it was the leg that had been crippled. Under the Dreambiter's attack, it was starting to draw up, pull back against her chest. Thistle's trembling was giving way to twitches and jerks that she couldn't control. Each was more violent than the one before.

Ratha was ready to fight, but the enemy was invisible, inside. The only thing she could see was Thistle herself, eyes swirling, slender body shuddering, mouth wide in a silent, agonized cry.

No . . . enemy.

But there is one. The Dreambiter.

Who is the Dreambiter, Ratha?

Mine and hers, yet it doesn't belong to either of us alone. Thakur said that it would take both of us to put it to rest.

He didn't say that both of us might have to die.

"Thistle," Ratha said softly, then nudged her daughter very gently, for fear of startling her.

The eyes turned to her. They were all swirling sea-green, like the ocean's clashing waves. The pupils had shrunk to the size of a claw point, swallowed by the wild storm within.

A spasm seized the once-crippled foreleg, jerking it, threatening to break the fragile clawhold of the foot. Ratha slapped her paw on top of Thistle's, drove her own, longer claws into the crumbling rock. She pushed hard, flattening Thistle's foot and keeping it there despite the continuing spasms in the leg.

"Bites," Thistle gasped. "Keeps biting. Won't stop. Wants . . . wants to kill."

The words tore into Ratha, making a wound in which pain welled up. But something else rose as well. A realization. Yes. The Dreambiter does want to kill. And I know why. When I attacked Thistle, out of rage and frustration and fear, I wanted to kill.

Now she knew. That is why the Dreambiter is so powerful.

Thistle was speaking again in a quavering voice. "Two Dreambiters. One inside. One outside."

Again the word hurt. More than Ratha could bear, and again she wanted to flee. Not back up the cliff to safety, but deep into the refuge of denial.

That wasn't me who bit you. That was something else. Someone else. That wasn't me, Thistle. It was an evil thing that came from outside, that wore my skin, looked through my eyes.

And because it wasn't me, it became the Dreambiter.

I said then that you made it. Even now I want to believe that you made it.

Two Dreambiters?

No, Thistle. There is only one. I am the Dreambiter, the Dreamkiller. But I am also the Dreamsaver, the

Dreamcarer. The same passion that drove me close to killing you has now driven me here, down onto this cliff. To either save you or die with you.

She is here. The one who gave me birth, who nearly gave me death. She is here.

Shadow teeth drive into chest and leg. Shadow teeth, but real pain, real wounds. The leg shrinks, crippled. Or it tries to, but something holds the paw from pulling back.

Teeth take hold of the scruff. Real teeth. Brace for more pain, Thistle. The real teeth are the ones that cast the shadows.

But . . . no pain. Not a bite. A hold. A mouth that held a very small cub.

She held me that way. I remember. She carried me that way. In that mouth, in those teeth that did not bite, there was gentleness, there was caring. When she carried me, I was safe. Nothing could harm me. All my legs were strong. All things were good and promising.

The Dreambiter drove it all away.

But now she has brought it back.

I remember. I remember. I felt it then. I feel it again now. In the gentleness of the jaws that hold my scruff. In the strength of the paw that holds my leg from drawing back. In the voice that says she will stay with me now, no matter what happens.

The pain in my leg has changed. It is not less than it used to be. It is worse, because my legs can't pull back. Bad enough so that I could scream. But it no longer has the bleakness and coldness that made me so helpless. It is a hot, wild pain, but one I can fight.

She is with me. All of her. In a way I have always wanted.

Leader of the Named. Tamer of the Red Tongue. Fighter for the clan.

Wounder and wounded. Singer and sung-to. Dreambiter and Dreambitten.

Ratha. My mother.

The fit that seized Thistle was bad enough, but Ratha, her jaws fastened in her daughter's scruff, dreaded even more what would happen when the attack ended. When the illness released its hold, Thistle would collapse into unconsciousness.

Ratha felt the driving beat of her heart in her breast where her fur met Thistle's. If she lets go, I won't be able to hold her. We'll both go down. I won't give up my hold. Not now.

She pressed against Thistle's foot more firmly than ever, making sure that her daughter kept at least one set of claws anchored. At any instant, she feared, the rigid, jerking body would either throw both of them from their precarious hold on the cliff face, or she would feel the sudden sag of Thistle's limbs as she toppled loose from the grip of the fit.

To her astonishment, neither happened. As she was bracing to somehow take Thistle's full weight, she realized that she no longer had to struggle to keep Thistle's foreleg extended or her pad pressed against the rock. The jerking spasms had died away. Thistle was holding on again, by herself.

"Am all right now," said the quiet little voice.

The wave of relief that washed over Ratha made her

own limbs weak, and she had to pay attention to keep her own clawhold on the rocks.

It was not until she felt Thistle moving that she remembered that she still was holding her by the scruff. Thankfully she released her grip and opened her jaws, which were now starting to ache.

She watched as Thistle, her agility regained, turned herself around to head back up the cliff face. As Thistle brushed her, she felt a grateful nudge and heard her daughter's voice saying softly, "Good-bye, Dreambiter. Welcome, Ratha-mother. Climb up carefully with me. True-of-voice needs both of us."

Ratha had a few bad moments while turning around, but by following Thistle's claw marks, she managed to get herself facing up the cliff. Her heart was still slamming inside her ribs, so hard that she thought it might shake her off, but the beat of dread and anger had been replaced by one of joy.

First Thistle and then Ratha reached the narrow, sloping ledge that led back to the top. Ratha saw Thakur reach down with a helping paw, first for Thistle and then herself.

Only when both were back on firm and stable ground did Ratha begin to feel her legs shake so hard that she sank down on her belly.

"You stay, Ratha-mother," Thistle said, pushing her firmly with a paw when she tried to overcome the shakiness and get up. Biaree, who had scrambled up onto Thistle's back, added a few treeling admonitions.

"My fur hasn't started to go gray yet, Thistle," Ratha protested, but she was grateful for the chance to take a brief rest.

"Both of you rest," said Thakur, butting Thistle gently off her feet so that she roiled over beside her mother. Biaree chittered, scolding Thakur.

"But True-of-voice—" Ratha tried.

"Is being taken care of. While you were down getting the vines tied onto him, Quiet Hunter was persuading his people to help us. A task that in some ways," Thakur added, "was as difficult as what you had to do."

Ratha saw her daughter's head turn sharply toward Quiet Hunter. The young male was well named. He was gentle and quiet in everything he said and did, but underlying the gentleness was a strong determination.

He had lined the hunters up near the cliff edge. Ratha saw that they were ready to take the heavy vine ropes in their mouths and lift True-of-voice off the ledge. Bira and Khushi were also working with Quiet Hunter. They were getting the rope holders arranged in relays so that the vine ropes could be carefully passed from one set of jaws to the next.

In some ways Quiet Hunter is the real leader of this group, Ratha thought. True-of-voice may have the gift of the song, but Quiet Hunter has a way of inspiring trust.

When her shakiness retreated enough so that she could creep back to the cliff edge and peer over, she saw that the rescue was already underway.

One problem immediately became apparent. The cliff edge was not an overhang that would have allowed the rescuers to raise True-of-voice by just pulling up on freely dangling ropes. There was a backward slant to the rock face, and the edge itself had been worn and broken. The ropes could not be allowed to rub against the rocks as they passed over the edge, or the vines would fray and tear.

Thakur and Quiet Hunter solved the difficulty, with more cooperation from the hunters themselves. By lying on their backs, pushing the vine ropes up off the ground with their paws, they protected the lines against damage and allowed them to slide slowly but freely. Several of True-of-voice's people even draped themselves over the edge, their companions hanging onto their forepaws, in order to use their powerful hind legs to cantilever the lines away from the cliff.

Soon True-of-voice was suspended by the vines that had been tied by treeling hands.

Ratha felt Thistle come alongside her, with Biaree still onboard.

"Treeling tied good knots," Thistle said, giving her companion an affectionate nudge. "Nothing slipped." She paused, then yowled at Thakur, who was helping Quiet Hunter. "Tell those fur-brained furballs not to bite down so hard. Will break the ropes!"

Ratha grinned to herself. Talk about leadership. She had a good idea who would probably be leading the clan when her fur did go gray and her muzzle turned white. Thistle's even bossier than I am.

Slowly, carefully, True-of-voice was lifted, then lowered past the ledge where he'd been trapped. The teams of rope holders kept the lines securely anchored, yet allowed them to slip.

"Easier if we had treeling paws," Thistle said, watching. "But using teeth works too. Wouldn't want to be where True-of-voice is now, though. Had enough of hanging off rocks."

Ratha narrowed her eyes, wondering if True-of-voice was alert enough to be aware of what was going on. She thought she had seen his eyes flutter open briefly. But he was either aware enough or unconscious enough not to struggle.

Just don't die before we get you to the bottom. And don't die then either.

As the vine-roped form descended, the hunters who had been moping at the foot of the cliff gathered and waited, their heads lifted, their eyes filled with wonder and hope.

And then came the moment when the ropes went slack because their burden had reached the ground. A weary team of rescuers, Named and hunters alike, turned to one another with relieved expressions. Below, at the foot of the cliff, the ones who had been keeping vigil now crowded in around their leader.

Thakur came to Ratha with Quiet Hunter. They crouched beside Ratha as Thakur said, "I'm going down there with him. Have you recovered enough to go with us?"

In answer, Ratha sprang to her feet. "We'd better hurry before they kill him with happiness. Thistle, you come, too. But watch your treeling."

She saw a look of pleased surprise come over her daughter's face.

Yes, I'm going to treat you as an equal now, so get used to it.

Once all the tumultuous greetings had died down, the hunters stood aside so that the Named and their healer could get to True-of-voice. At the bottom of the cliff,

Ratha watched, wondering if all the effort had been for nothing or whether True-of-voice would survive.

Thakur worked devotedly over the hunting clan's leader while others of the Named ran back and forth, gathering the herbs he asked for.

"He's pretty battered, Ratha," Thakur said when he paused briefly in his efforts, "but there are no severe wounds. What nearly killed him was lack of water."

He spent the rest of the day and most of the night tending True-of-voice, while both the Named and the hunters kept a quiet but hopeful vigil.

Their patience was rewarded when a weary Thakur at last came to Ratha and said that True-of-voice would take several days to recover his strength, but he was out of danger. When Ratha had Quiet Hunter announce it to his people, there were yowls of joy.

Her gaze went to Thistle and Quiet Hunter, standing on each side of Thakur and helping to keep the herding teacher from falling over out of sheer exhaustion.

The two did not join in the outburst of celebration, but Ratha could tell by the looks they exchanged that they were the happiest of all.

Thistle is not the only one who can cross over between the two peoples. Quiet Hunter, who can swim in the bright and bubbling flow of the song, can also walk the trails of the Named.

The gift the Named have given to the hunters is the words that they have taught.

Understanding. Acceptance. Wisdom.

In both clans.

The song is heard.

* * *

There had never been such a meeting between the Named and outsiders before, Ratha thought. The same was true for the hunters, or so True-of-voice said. Ratha had received the information through Thistle and Quiet Hunter. She had not yet spoken directly to True-of-voice at any length, although she had exchanged brief words with him while he lay under Thakur's care.

The meeting took place on the open grassy plain. Each of the two tribes sat in a semicircle around its leader. Both leaders had someone special at their sides. Beside Ratha sat Thistle, her eyes clear, her ears up, and a treeling perched on her shoulder. Across from Ratha was True-of-voice, the massive gray male who was more than just a leader to those who clustered about him. Beside True-of-voice sat Quiet Hunter.

The two who can cross over to the others' trails. The messengers. The sinews that bind our tribes together.

Among the Named were those who had not been on the initial search for face-tails. Beside Thakur in the half circle of the Named sat Fessran and others who had been summoned to be present.

The excited buzz that was running through both sides of the circle died down. As if it were a signal, both Thistle and Quiet Hunter rose, their gazes fixed on each other. Ratha knew that for these two, little else existed right now. The bond between her daughter and the shy son of the hunting group was far more than the mating of male and female. Thistle and Quiet Hunter shared experiences that none of their people had known. Each had had to break out of a familiar way of being and risk those things that they valued most. Now both were being rewarded.

As Thistle and Quiet Hunter came together and touched noses, Ratha felt that something new had been born—a feeling deeper than any that could be felt by members of either tribe alone. When she looked across to True-of-voice, she knew that he realized the same thing, for his gaze was also fixed on the young pair.

True-of-voice. I have wondered about him. I have hated him. Now I am about to know him.

Thistle and Quiet Hunter came first to Ratha, one flanking her on each side.

"I am still a little afraid," Ratha said in a low voice to her daughter.

"Everyone here is also. That is where the bravery is," Thistle answered. "You are brave enough, Rathamother."

The daughter of the Named and the son of the hunters brushed close to Ratha on either side as they escorted her to the center point of the full circle made up by the two tribes. The pair then went to True-of-voice, took up positions to either side of him, and brought the leader forward.

Ratha watched him approach, her heart beating hard with a mixture of trepidation and hope. He and she were so different. His people and the Named were so alien to each other. How could it possibly work?

Yet, looking at Thistle and Quiet Hunter, she knew that it could. With enough wisdom . . . and bravery . . . on both sides.

She extended her head for the nose-touch, breathed

in True-of-voice's breath, and gave hers to be breathed in by him.

What is it like to walk in a dream with your people? To be center and soul to them? To be the wellspring of the song?

He's probably asking himself what it is like to be me, how I can be leader to a bunch of stubborn characters who not only know their own names but think for themselves whether I want them to or not!

True-of-voice, I don't think we are that different after all.

Finding her voice, Ratha said, "We of the Named are here to join your people in friendship. We have talents that we will share, abilities that we will teach, if your tribe wishes."

"The value of those things has been shown," answered True-of-voice. "The Named saved this life, this song, this people. Named gifts will be accepted with joy and things given in return."

She listened as he proposed the kinds of exchanges that would help both tribes. The Named would be allowed to take face-tails and add them to their herds if they so wished. If they needed help, the hunters would provide it. In return, the hunters might wish to adopt Named herding skills and learn about some of the other herdbeasts, such as the three-horn deer and dapplebacked horses.

There was also interest in treelings. The continued presence of Biaree on Thistle's shoulder, as she went among the members of the hunting tribe, had sparked curiosity. Ratha noticed that True-of-voice's people went to great lengths to make sure that the treeling was never alarmed or threatened.

Biaree was now Thistle's. Ratha had not intended it to happen, but somehow the bond that had formed between her daughter and the treeling during the rescue of True-of-voice was deeper and stronger than the one that Bira, Biaree's original companion, had built.

Ratha glanced over at Bira. The little ruddy-coated Firekeeper looked proud, yet there was a sadness in her eyes. She had been with Biaree since the treeling's birth, carefully training him in the skills that she and he both needed to carry out the duties demanded by the Red Tongue. And then, in only a few days, she had lost him to Thistle.

It was a measure of Bira's clear-sightedness that she had been the one to suggest that the temporary arrangement be made permanent. Biaree could have come back to her, for he had kept his affection for his first companion. But what had been created between Thistle and the treeling had a seriousness and a depth that went beyond the usual treeling-Named bond. Perhaps having a life at stake had increased the two partners' devotion to each other.

I will make sure that Bira gets the first choice of the next treeling litter. As Thistle said, everyone is showing bravery, and Bira is not the least.

As Ratha gazed at her daughter, she realized that the change inside Thistle was starting to change her outside.

She's not so scruffy anymore. She's filling out a bit. And when she grooms her coat, she's really quite pretty.

The meeting was starting to wind down. True-of-voice was making one last suggestion, one he was sure that the Named would agree to.

Thistle and Quiet Hunter would be allowed to move freely from one tribe to the other, staying together and using their combined skills to aid the members of both tribes to understand one another. There would be disagreements, perhaps even open conflicts. That was inevitable between peoples as different as theirs. But with two who could walk both sets of trails, there would be a better chance that matters could be settled without fighting.

We are setting out on another journey—one I never thought we'd ever take. But it feels right.

It happened because of you, Thistle. I never knew that daughters could help their mothers grow up. You yourself may be a mother some day. You already are, in a sense. A mother to two tribes of quarreling cubs that are also learning.

You have more than I ever hoped. A place. A purpose. A treeling companion to comfort you. And another companion, if I am any judge of what Quiet Hunter wants. He will be a gentle, devoted mate, I think. He is what you need.

And there is also . . .

One who is still struggling to find the best ways. Not only for myself and the Named, but for others as well.

A clan leader, a Dreambiter, a Dreamhealer. Impatient, reckless, carrier of fire, bearer of cubs. Jumping into unknown abysses, scrambling up dangerous cliffs. Facing challenges—and the greatest one is you.

You have a new name for me now.

Ratha-mother.